NIGHTMARES' NEST

By Kenneth O'Hara

NIGHTMARES' NEST

KENNETH O'HARA

PUBLISHED FOR THE CRIME CLUB BY
DOUBLEDAY & COMPANY, INC.
GARDEN CITY, NEW YORK
1983

The only characters in this novel who are not wholly fictitious are the horses.

Library of Congress Cataloging in Publication Data

O'Hara, Kenneth.
Nightmares' Nest.

I. Title.
PR6065.H28N5   1983   823'.914
ISBN 0-385-18842-0
Library of Congress Catalog Card Number 82-25165

NIGHTMARES' NEST

CHAPTER 1

There had been a message-board in the tack-room, with a drawing-pinned list of the day's riders and a bulldog clip holding a half-used pad scrawled with requests and reminders. It was not until the Saturday, two days after the murder at Stumbletts Farm, that Sergeant Cheal noticed the faint line in the glued top of this pad, and took it from its clip. It had been cut in two like a pack of cards, so that the front sheet was now in the middle. On this sheet was written:

The Killers are out again.

By that time they had marked out the lines of their investigation. After thought Hobden said mildly, "That's something we didn't expect."

"*Again?*" said Cheal. "But that's nonsense!" He had his own view on the Stumbletts murder, and was working on it. Hobden did not agree with it, and they were working on that too. What they did agree on was that the two views were the only possible ones, and that if one was not right then the other was. "*Again* would mean that this isn't the first death. And it is! We don't have murders in these villages." As a C.I.D. sergeant and a native of the villages he was doubly outraged.

"There was a manslaughter," said Hobden, "—twenty-two years back, was it?" He was a benevolent elderly man, coming up to retiring age, who lived just outside the town and had a busy wife much taken up with local charities; but his patch included the wicked mile on the coast and the racecourses, and there his reputation was not for benevolence. He examined the sheet ruminatively. "Italic handwriting; might be a child's. Some kids' game. Likely nothing to do with it at all."

He was only partly right. The message had been written by Benjamin Cullen; but not even Benjamin knew that in it he had touched on the begetting of the Stumbletts murder.

The emergency call had come at ten-fifteen on the Friday morning, from a very shaken young woman. She had given her name as Diana Aubrey, with an address in Chelsea, but had stammered so much over what she had to report that an older, steadier voice had abruptly taken over.

"Mrs. Cullen of Stumbletts Farm. You know it?—on the main coast road just your side of Hole Lane. The riding school, yes, that's it. One of the girl grooms has been found dead in a stable; murdered, we think. Can you help us, please? Thank you, yes, we haven't moved anything. But—if you wouldn't mind—"

"Yes, Mrs. Cullen?"

"We have five young children here, riding pupils of Mrs. Brooke. Would it be possible not to let them know what's happened? We can't get their parents here at once."

Since the children were between nine and twelve, the presence of parents would be necessary. Hobden said,

"Tell her to get them as soon as she can." The only buses that ran through the town these days were the fast ones to the coast, and there were none that served the surrounding villages, so he did not expect this to be very soon; but even less did he expect to arrive at Stumbletts to find everything arranged over his head.

"Not a farm these days," Cheal had told him briefly on the way. "Used to be thirty acres, mostly dairy, but Ben Cullen was killed in a tractor accident four years ago; widow tried to carry on, but couldn't with two young children; leased the land to her brother-in-law down the road, keeps going running a farm shop. Then she leased the farm buildings to that Mrs. Brooke down Hole Lane. Wait a bit, there are two gates; first one's the riding school, second the farm. Pull in at the first."

But the gate which carried the notice STUMBLETTS STABLES was closed, and as the car drew up a tall woman in jeans unlatched it just far enough to admit one person.

"Would you be awfully kind and stay out there for a few minutes?"

Hobden got out. "Detective Chief Inspector Hobden, ma'am. We received a telephone call—"

"Valentine Brooke. How do you do. Do come in, but could you please be kind and leave your men and car outside for ten minutes? We are just getting the children out on their ride. We want this to be as little of a shock as possible."

"I appreciate that, ma'am. But I'm afraid I shall have to interview them all."

"Of course you will, though they arrived together at five to ten and there are two of us to assure you that they never went near that building over the yard there, where the dead girl is. And aren't I right, you'll need their parents present? We are telephoning to have them collected, but they've all come for the day and some of the parents aren't at home. Now of course you can shut them up in the farmhouse and let them get thoroughly wrought up, but wouldn't it be more convenient to let me send them out on the hour's ride they came for and come quietly back to be picked up?"

This was the first of Hobden's many differences with Valentine Brooke. She was in her late forties, with a straight rider's back, a pony-crop of greying yellow hair, and a smiling cat face with narrow dark eyes like caraway seeds. However wrong-headed he thought her (and he never knew the half of it, and suspected so), he could not fault her practical arrangements. He gave way gracefully and directed his car to pull in in the shelter of the tall hedge between the two gates, turning a quelling eye on Cheal's expression.

"That's very kind indeed," said Valentine Brooke. "Come and see the place while you wait."

"The dead girl, ma'am?"

"In that building there, shut and bolted as we found it this morning." It was a shed on the other side of the yard, next to another labelled *Tack-Room*. The yard was paved and roomy, with a Dutch barn on one side, and, shielding the farmhouse, the back of a long barn on the other. "My small stable. Indoor school, tack-room, yard, and the big stable round the side there, they're mine. The girl's name is Jill Edmonds; she's fifteen, a schoolgirl from Seaford, and was staying with me at Hole Cottage. I came here this morning just before ten, with Diana Aubrey and two horses, to get ready for my first ride at ten-thirty, opened the small stable to show Diana the horse in there, and saw her; you'll see how. I lifted one hand to be sure she was dead, but let it back as it lay. Otherwise I've touched nothing except to put a sheet over her and cross over, well by the wall, to my horse. He's still in there but I've tied him up; he's nervous, but I couldn't lead him out without disturbing Ji—without disturbing the body. Speak to him when you go in, but don't get close." Her voice was hard and matter-of-fact; it shifted at once to a throaty briskness as a small child burst from the tackroom cramming on a riding-hat. "Move, Tina, they're in the big stable."

The child swerved at full speed round the end of the big stable, and Valentine followed her. The farmhouse was on the far side of this yard, the old dairy by the road stacked around its door with boxes of tomatoes and stone jars full of cut flowers. The noise inside the big stable came to them abruptly; it had hardly been audible in the stable yard.

"Here's Kit; the shop and farmhouse are hers. May I leave you with her? The children will think it odd if I don't see them mount. Mr. Hobden, Mrs. Cullen. Kit, what about your two?"

Kit Cullen was a small wiry woman, with a cap of curling coppery hair and a tanned face ten years older than her hair. She nodded briefly to Hobden. "I've told them they can go out with the ride—that okay? They've taken bridles into the field to bring in Mouse and Cupid." She gave Hobden a grudging look. "My son and daughter. I'd like them out of the way; they're too damned sharp."

Valentine went to the door of the big stable, around which was a crowd of children and ponies. "They'll go out of my back gate," Kit supplied, "and across the common and on to the old road. I've only managed to find one mother, but she can take all five; they all share transport anyway; she'll be here about noon."

"You don't send them out alone?"

"No, of course not. Oh, Val missed telling you. She has two grooms. Damn. I have to say she had, haven't I?

That's the other one there, in the blue T-shirt, mounting little Tina."

A round-faced girl, with nut-brown hair tied out of the way, was tossing up the small child with a slap on the bottom.

"Jonty Barton. You'll want to talk to her, I suppose. I've rung her parents to come over already, because Jill was her great friend. She doesn't know yet. At least," Kit corrected herself after a long look at the girl, "she doesn't know she's dead. She knows something; or why isn't she looking for Jill to help her?"

By the stable-door, Valentine was thinking the same. Mild as always, Jonty was saying above the chatter, "Girths, everyone, check your girths before you mount." She did not demand, "Where's that lazy cow?" She did not even look at Valentine with her wide bee-stung brows questioningly lifted. She did not look at Valentine at all; yes, Jonty knew. She would be suspecting an accident; Jill schooled the new horse every morning, and was careless about wearing a hat.

"Tracey, stirrup's wrong way again, and Jane will need a whip with Gingerbread. Someone mount Karen, please."

A good worker, Jonty; clinging to it now against the panic of disaster; her voice was faintly shrill. Karen had let down a stirrup to mount the fifteen-hand Robert, and failed; her sister Jane left Gingerbread to stand and linked hands to help her.

"—after the last ride of the day," Kit was saying in the yard outside. "Half past six or so, and when she locks up—"

She puts the dog on guard, Valentine completed automatically to herself.

The Alsatian Dandy was Kit's dog. In the daytime he lived with her. At night, from his bed by the stable gate, he guarded the stable yard. When he was there, no stranger could enter the yard.

When Valentine was deeply shocked, she did not jump, but froze. From her stance by the door, hands in pockets, no one could mark her sudden cold rigidity. As soon as she could move steadily, she took two steps sideways into the shovel that stood against the wall.

It went over with a clang, and every pony jumped. Amanda's Fox shied out into the yard, Amanda squealing, and as Jane grasped at Gingerbread Karen was left on her stomach across Robert's saddle.

"Shut up and get up," Jonty said, unruffled, and heaved her up. Valentine pushed past noses and took Fox's bridle, saying, "Sorry, loves, stepped on the shovel. Amanda, he wouldn't have done that if you'd been ready for him. Look, you nearly had Kit down. And, Jane, I'm sorry but you can't ride Gingerbread, he's going lame. Help Jonty get his tack off. Kit—Kit, sorry to interrupt, but will you help me with Snowgoose?"

She snatched saddle and bridle into the back stall where the little Appaloosa mare stood. Jane lamented and unbuckled Gingerbread's girth. Kit pushed and ducked her way into the back stall. Valentine eased the saddle on to the mare's back and stooped under her belly to be handed the girth. In that shelter she muttered fiercely to Kit, *"Don't mention Dandy."*

She came up from the buckle to find Kit staring at her. She eased the bit into the mare's mouth, buckled the throat-latch, and led her out.

"Right, Jane. Right, everyone? Out the full hour, Jonty, and straight back in here afterwards."

Jonty looked away from her. "Tina, you're riding too short, stirrups down two holes." She vaulted on to the tall black Ebony, and, one hand on the rump to watch them, led them out by the back gate. From the meadow at her back two ponies came at a hard canter to fall in behind, Benjamin and Bridie Cullen, riding bareback.

"And now, Mr. Hobden," said Valentine, turning to him with a sigh. Kit was not visible.

CHAPTER 2

"And now, ma'am," said Hobden much later.

They had sat silent in Kit's big kitchen while the police went about their business. Valentine had at once seized the coffee-pot and filled it, but after that did nothing but stare from the window. Kit, grim-faced, got out her workbasket and started mending. Diana Aubrey, who was twenty and a stranger to Stumbletts, sat quietly for some time, and then, a little shyly, reached for a thimble and joined her. All the time a constable stood solidly outside the open door.

From the kitchen, the length of the big stable hid the stable yard. They heard cars coming and going; once Valentine made a small noise and they saw the white nose of an ambulance as it turned. At the end of the hour, a clatter of hooves and bursts of laughter marked the return of the ride. Kit at once got up.

"Mr. Hobden's there, ma'am," said the constable.

"And so are my son and daughter," said Kit, and walked past him.

Valentine stood by the window and sombrely watched the children clatter into the yard, dismount, and start untacking. Hobden came to join Kit, and a shabby estate car nosed in; Mary Rolands put her head out of the window and spoke at length and crossly. Hobden went to her; Kit dealt with the children, who attempted to carry their saddles round into the tack-room; Jonty moved mildly among them all, her round face untroubled, undoing stiff buckles, heaving off high saddles. Mary Rolands' ingenuous face expressed her struggle between intense curiosity and the instinct to keep away from trouble. The five children were packed into her car and driven away. Benjamin and Bridie, hanging urgently around Kit, were sent indoors sharply, and burst in with a stare at the constable.

"Val, what's up? Mum says we're to stay in. Why can't we go out? Why have we got the fuzz here?"

Valentine stirred herself to say, "Ask your mum later. Just now, be useful and do as she says."

"Yes, but I ought to be schooling Florian, and Bridie—"

"Benjamin: just try to be helpful, will you?"

Benjamin was small for his age, and thus Napoleonic; he stood scowling. Bridie, a copper-haired bunch with missing front teeth, smiled sweetly on them and dragged him away. Valentine turned back to the window; but the yard was empty.

Kit came in, very sharp. "Kids in their room?"

"Where's Jonty?"

"It's all right. I've told her about Jill."

"Bless you. What did she say?"

"Nothing. Looked at me and nodded. That Hobden wanted to send her to sit in here and get the horrors. I persuaded him to let her get on with the stable-work. He wants you, Val. The new horse has to come out of the small stable."

Valentine looked at her wonderingly. "I forgot him," she said. "I forgot a horse."

There was no one in the small stable now but Hobden, standing looking ruminatively around him.

"I hope he's been all right?"

"A bit restive at first, but one of my men took a fancy to him and got him calm. He's a handsome fellow."

He was a fifteen-two gelding, cream with a wild blue eye. Untying him, Valentine said absently, "Not settled in yet, so we left him in here. Horses always bully a new-comer. I suppose you *have* worked out that Jill died before midnight?"

Hobden took a close look at her, and said, "We haven't seen a medical report yet. What makes you think that, ma'am?"

"Well, you've only my word for it. The water-bucket there. I know how much my horses drink. This cream was out yesterday afternoon, so he would have drunk at the trough when he came in, and not been thirsty again until around midnight. But he wouldn't have touched tainted water, and the bucket's still full."

She led out the cream, crossing the yard round to the big stable. At the sound of hooves Jonty came to the door.

"Want him in here?" she said offhandedly. "Oke, I'll take him." Taking hold of the head-collar she effectively turned her back on Valentine. Her favourite mount, the lazy chestnut Gingerbread, was out of his stall; he had been brushed until he gleamed, and his mane and tail were being plaited.

"And now, ma'am. Perhaps you'll tell us what you can about this unfortunate business. Starting perhaps with your discovery of the body?"

Valentine rubbed her forehead. "I think that goes back to last night."

"Just in your own words."

"Because I thought Jill was in. In bed, I mean. In my house."

"You employed her?"

"Part-time. She and Jonty are—were—are still at school. I paid them board and lodging and pocket-money, with all the riding they wanted, for all the time they liked to come, which was, roughly speaking, all their spare time. Transport's hard from their homes, so at week-ends and holidays they use my spare bedrooms."

"I see. And you thought she was in last night? What time was this?"

"She came in about a quarter to nine. They were going to the disco at the Youth Club, but decided against it when they got there and instead went to a friend's house and played records. That's Jill, Jonty, Jonty's boy-friend John, who's old enough to drive his father's car, and this girl Fiona and her brother. Jill didn't like Fiona and walked back to my place—it's only ten minutes' walk along Church Lane. I was doing my books in front of the television, and Jill watched for a minute or two and then decided it was boring and went into the kitchen for a snack."

"You heard her there?"

"No, my doors are solid. But I heard her take two telephone calls, and the bookings were on the pad when I went to bed. I take most of my bookings by telephone in the evenings. Oh yes—she looked in once to ask if we had horses to spare for three extra on Saturday. I asked was she going to bed, to know if I should take any other calls, and she said she was doing some ironing. I noticed it this morning—three shirts and some jeans: say three-quarters of an hour's work."

"You didn't see or hear her again?"

"I sort of took it that I did," Valentine said after reflection. "Jonty came in about twenty to eleven; her John's a reliable boy and is always punctual. She came in to me and said something or other about her evening. Then she decided to make cocoa, and I heard her shout upstairs to know if Jill wanted any. I supposed she'd been answered, because when she brought me my cocoa she said she'd locked up and was going to bed."

"And you went to bed yourself then?"

"After the late news. Both bedroom doors were shut then. You can't see when the lights are on, but shutting the door was their recognized do-not-disturb sign."

"So Jill could easily have slipped out quietly?"

"If you mean surreptitiously, she could, but I don't think she would. I insisted they should tell me their transport arrangements, and what time they'd be home, but otherwise I never asked what they were doing; consequently they told me. If Jill had wanted to go out I'd have asked if she wanted driving there."

"But if she had intended staying out longer than you would allow—"

Valentine looked at him in a kind of despair. "It sounds all right; it sounds just the sort of thing a fifteen-year-old girl would do, doesn't it? I know I've no hope of persuading you differently, but just let me remind you that I know—knew—the girl better than anyone, except perhaps Jonty; and I don't believe it for a moment."

"Noted, ma'am," Hobden said gravely.

"Anyway, the point's not relevant. She could have gone out in the most open way in the world and I could have missed it. I had the door shut, and though the window was open it faces the wrong way. The girls went in and out a lot in the summer evenings. We're a neighbourly lot around Hollow Cross, and the girls knew everyone. They borrowed records and hairdriers, and went up to old Mr. Unsted with tack to repair, and called at the back door of the shops for things they'd forgotten in legal opening hours. Jill could have done any of those things; she could simply have taken a walk on a fine evening. The one thing I wouldn't expect her to do was to come here."

"She wouldn't call on Mrs. Cullen?"

"No. Kit's too busy and Jill didn't get on with her all that well."

"The horse, ma'am?"

"Horse?"

"In the stable where she was found."

"Oh—the blue-eyed cream. Oh, she wouldn't have come for him. I was telling you about him, wasn't I? He'd been mishandled before I bought him. The usual story, silly family who hadn't a rider strong enough to handle him, and wanted to get rid of him because they said he was unrideable. The one thing you must do to settle a horse in a new home is to get him into a routine, and our routine is to leave them alone from seven in the evening until ten. Jill was attached to that cream; I'd turned him over to her, and she was bringing him on wonderfully well. She'd never have unsettled him by disturbing him."

"Yet she did go into the stable, ma'am," Hobden reminded her.

"Yes, I was thinking about that. If she was here, he'd have recognized her step and her voice, and start moving about; and then she'd go in to him. But he wasn't a reason for her to come here."

Hobden made a lengthy note. He wrote in longhand, carefully and not very fast, with many paragraphs and blank lines. "So we come to this morning."

"Well," Valentine said a little blankly, "for me it was like any other morning. I got up first, just before seven, did some housework, had my breakfast, and left at about nine. I knew one of the girls was up because I could hear the bath-water running, but I didn't know which. They always stay in bed until the last possible moment, and I always—I mean, I used to leave the coffee-pot and toaster ready for them."

"You came here separately?"

"That depended on whether there were horses to be fetched from out-grazing. Kit only has the home field, so I use a lot of out-grazing, wherever I can beg or rent it within three or four miles around. If it's as far as that, we leave together, and I drive the girls there and they bring the horses down: bareback to save the trouble of taking up saddles. This morning I had Diana Aubrey booked for the first ride, and she asked me if I could pick her up at her mother's house, so I took her on to my grazing and she drove my van here while I brought my two horses."

"And the girls would have walked?"

"Walk or bike. There's a floating population of bikes."

"Did it surprise you that Miss Barton arrived without realizing that her friend was missing?"

"Without mentioning to me that she was missing," Valentine corrected. "No, not a bit. They took turns for the bath, and the one without a bath would stay in bed a bit longer, and they never ate much breakfast. Since it must have been Jonty in the bath, she'd have come here as soon as she was ready, and assumed that Jill was doing the same."

"I see. Well, Miss Barton herself can sort that out for us. Her parents I know are on the way, but so far we haven't been able to get in touch with Mr. and Mrs. Edmonds at the telephone number you gave us."

"It is the holiday season."

"They wouldn't have let you know if they were going away? Considering that their daughter—"

Valentine hesitated. "I don't want to—when they're not here—"

"Facts?" Hobden murmured discreetly.

"Oh, plenty. That they go on holiday frequently and

never have let either Jill or me know, let alone taken her with them. The family is a father, stepmother, and two young stepbrothers. Jill's mother died when she was four. I don't suggest any neglect in the legal sense, and whatever feeling there was I am quite sure that Jill returned pretty smartly; but what there was was a profound lack of interest and a rather shocking readiness to hand her over to me. The father's a tiny little man who seldom utters, the mother a head taller and twice his weight—no, Mr. Hobden, I am sticking to facts, I'm a qualified riding instructor and that means I can judge weights—and the boys are attractive and spoilt. When I first offered Jill riding lessons and transport in exchange for stable-work, that was nearly four years ago and I said I must see her mother first. Jill very reluctantly gave me a telephone number, and the woman said yes without even seeing me, without even demanding a reference. I have only seen them once, and that was when the two girls decided to move in on me in the holidays to save transport. I made a proper arrangement with the Bartons, and finally went to Seaford and tackled the Edmondses. They simply agreed to anything I said; would hardly even attend. The only remark I got out of the stepmother was that at least it would stop the girl getting into bad company."

Hobden asked mildly, "And did it, ma'am?"

Valentine sat back in her seat. "I knew we'd come to that. You can consult police records, can't you? You won't find her there. Not for any reasons of profound virtue— I'm not flying to Jill's defence regardless. But to get into bad company you have to have a taste for company at all, and that Jill never had. What everyone else did was the one thing she would never do. And after she came to me— oh, good, we're back on to facts again—after she came to me I could account for almost every moment of her time. I wasn't paying her at first, and she needed a hat, and then boots and jodhs, so she took another part-time job, and having discovered that she was a natural with horses she took one Jonty found her with horses, and of course I knew the people she worked for, and heard a great deal about her. I can give you their name, if you want to check that. Then they started here as grooms in earnest, and I can tell you that if a girl works from breakfast till supper at hard physical work, and can't get more than a bicycle-ride away by herself in the few hours that are left to her, she has very little chance of getting into any company at all. One thing about the shocking lack of public transport here: we do know where our children are, because we have to drive them there and collect them afterwards."

"You say you employed her as a groom, but also taught her to ride."

"No, I didn't say so. When I was teaching her to ride I only asked her for general help, which was mostly muck-ing-out. That was a pretence anyway, not to lose such a talent. If you want to hear about that?"

Hobden nodded.

"Well, you'll have to wait a minute." They were in Kit's parlour, which Hobden had taken over as an office. Val-entine wandered around it for a time, and finally pounced into a drawer. "This is the end of it," she remarked, com-ing back to her seat with a packet of cigarettes. "Of my stopping smoking, I mean. Now I shall have to go through stopping all over again." She took a long pull and sighed. "Well: it was when I was only vaguely thinking of starting this school. My son had gone to university, and I had time on my hands and not a lot of money. I'd taught before he was born, and even after that always managed to have something to do with horses, filling in for friends, teaching neighbours' children, schooling awk-ward horses; I'd even managed to keep a couple of ponies myself so that I could teach my son. I couldn't afford full-

time help and was looking out for someone part-time—a
mother who'd ridden as a child seemed the best bet. Well,
Ted Barton rang me one day about a big gelding that
wanted schooling, and said he'd get one of his boys to
ride it over. In fact it was Jonty who did that, because she
had heard I was thinking of starting up and was after a
job. What no one had told Ted was that the horse
spooked at heavy lorries, and though Jonty was a very capable rider even then she hadn't the weight to hold him.
All I knew was that the horse turned up here with two
very tired girls hanging on to him, and I took it that Jonty
had brought a friend to help. The moment I turned my
back, there was Jill on my Barnaby, who's a blood pony
and a mass of nerves, coming up the old road at a canter
with her reins flapping loose round his heels and her
hands over her head, uttering cowboy yells. I asked her
pretty sharply why she hadn't knotted her reins before
she dropped them, and she said she hadn't dropped them,
she couldn't find them, because she'd never been on a
horse before. It turned out that she had been mooching
about on the road, seen Jonty in difficulty, and somehow
been moved to go and help; they'd never seen one another before. Well, I wasn't going to let slip a rider like
that, but when I mentioned lessons she shut up tight and
said she couldn't afford them, and anyway could only get
here by hitching. So I said pay for the lessons with some
stable-work, and Jonty in her quiet voice said she could
arrange transport and did I want two stable-workers? I
didn't take it too seriously to begin with, but they did.
Maybe because they were in on the school from rather
before the start, they've always been partners rather than
grooms."

Telling this story had cheered Valentine; her shoulders
straightened from their droop and her voice was lively.
Hobden studied her for a moment before he asked,

"How would you describe Jill, ma'am—as a person, not as a rider? If you can separate the two."

"I can't," Valentine said promptly. "A rider was what she was."

"I shall be seeing Miss Barton shortly. Was Jill like her, for example?"

"No, not a bit. I don't know how to describe Jonty, but whatever she is Jill isn't. *Damn,* wasn't; when shall I get used to saying that? It's almost impossible to upset Jonty or make her irritable; it was very difficult not to upset Jill. Not that she created; just closed up. Didn't handle people well. The young ones here admired her riding, of course, so she did well with them. Some of the older ones weren't too fond of her. She had an incredibly sharp eye for pretentiousness, and an equally sharp tongue, when she bothered to employ it. I don't think she had much interest in people. Jonty and I were part of the furniture of her life, so she liked us around; otherwise she preferred horses, I believe. Horses have their faults, but they aren't pretentious."

"Did she have no boy-friends?"

"Shoals. Many more than Jonty, who tends to be faithful to one for four or five months at a time. But she was never interested in them. They might have been her boy-friends, but she was never anyone's girl-friend."

"Ma'am," said Hobden heavily, "you can't be ignorant that in crimes of this type we have to investigate all contacts."

"And the first to be suspected are boy-friends: of course I know it. I can give you a list, which will probably include every boy of an appropriate age who has ever ridden here. Not non-riders: she didn't have time to make many contacts outside the stables, and it was her riding that attracted; if they didn't admire that, her moods put them off. And, making the next jump, I am willing to bet that you'll find she never slept with one of them."

Hobden said merely, "I'll be grateful for the list. Now I understand that you have some adult riders."

"Just a few. Pupils or liveries. The adult pupils are exceptions; sometimes they're past pupils, like Diana here, but mostly they're mothers of pupils. I have only three big horses, and of those only Harvey can carry a heavy man, which limits me. As for the liveries, I have to take them because they pay well. I charge as little as possible for lessons because I like to teach those who couldn't otherwise afford it; and there are plenty of those. We look after the livery horses, of course, but they go out independently of us."

"Are any of them men?"

"No. The men around here who ride are farmers, who have their own grazing and outbuildings and don't need a livery stable."

"Presumably some of the ladies are married?"

Valentine suppressed some words, and leaning sideways in her chair hauled something from her jeans pocket. "I think you'd better borrow this, Mr. Hobden."

It was a bent and shabby notebook, some crumbs of leather showing that it had once been morocco-bound. "In there you'll find the name, age, address, weight, and riding standard of everyone who has ever ridden here."

She was bleakly consoled by the fact that Hobden looked a little taken aback.

Stumbletts was a pleasant old house, but it bore the unmistakable marks of pinched means and pinched time. Diana Aubrey did not. Her boots matched her hair, her shirt and eye-shadow her eyes, and all were of the highest quality. But, even allowing for the fact that she was upset and out of her depth, she had a shyness that was appealing. What she had to add to Valentine's account of the morning was largely to do with herself and not very relevant.

"Yes, it was Val taught me to ride, ages ago; well, eight years ago. Well, she came to school my pony first, because he was too much for me. I'm not a very strong rider. I'd had lessons, of course, but I wasn't very confident, and I used to go hacking with her and Caspar—that's her son. When I went to London—I work in an art gallery in Chelsea—the pony was sold and I really gave up riding, but I came down for a holiday and thought I'd like to see Val again, and she persuaded me to come for a ride. Yes, I didn't bring my car down so I had to ask her to pick me up, and she rode her two horses down and I drove her van. We got here almost together because she took the short cut across from Church Lane while I had to go round by road. I drove in at Mrs. Cullen's gate; I don't think I should have done, but I've never been here before, and it was the only one that was open. Val was just dismounting and talking to Mrs. Cullen, and Jonty was tacking up in the big stable; I saw Jonty just for a second when Val smacked her two horses in to her. The stable gate was closed, I think; yes, because as Val and I went into the stable yard there was a car outside with the children, and Val shouted at them not to climb over the gate. The children, thank heaven, ran straight to the tack-room, to find out which horses they were riding, Val said. Val and I went to the small stable, because I'd heard she had a new horse and asked if I could see him. I've never heard his name, but she calls him the blue-eyed cream. The yard was quite tidy and swept, and the door bolted on the outside. Val was talking to me over her shoulder as we went in, about Jill schooling the cream, so that we were right inside before we saw—oh dear."

She made some pretty play with her long eyelashes, but had gone very pale.

"Now I know it's upsetting, miss, but if you could be helpful enough to tell us just what you saw—"

"It was so awful I expect I missed a lot. The blue-eyed cream was on the far side and Jill lying between him and the door; her head was towards him and turned to the left, so that we could see the right side, where the—where she'd been hit. There was blood splashed everywhere, on the floor and in the water-bucket and on that pile of anoraks and sweaters by the door. There was a rusty old horseshoe, a shire's I should think from the size, lying at her right side, with blood and dark hair on one end of it. . . . I think Val just said *Jill*—like that, quite quietly. Somehow it had never occurred to me that that was who it was. I didn't know her, you see, though I had heard of her."

"From Mrs. Brooke?"

"And I sometimes see Caspar in London. I suppose it was because she was in an obvious sort of party dress, except for her shoes, which were sandals that didn't match. But she was dead, obviously; I mean, with her head like that no one could have thought— And the blood was quite black. Val felt her hand, and said it was quite cold. And then we had to run out because the children were coming. Val shut the door behind us and told them to go into the tack-room and stay there. I know she seems casual, but I remember myself, if Val said to do something you did it. I stayed by the door to watch them while Val called Kit and told her what had happened. Kit said—"

"You heard all this?"

"Yes, Kit came into the stable yard. Kit said at once what about the children, meaning her two as well, who were somewhere around the farm, and Val said to find them and keep them out of the way while I telephoned.

She asked Kit to find a sheet to cover the—cover the body, and when we'd telephoned we went back with the sheet and Val was in the tack-room starting the children cleaning tack. She shut the door on them and put a bucket against it so that it would fall over and warn us if they came out, and we went into the small stable. I don't think Kit said a word, but she goes a terrible bluish pale. They put the sheet over Jill, and—oh yes, they were talking about Jonty. They were worried about telling her."

"Where was she all this time?"

"In the big stable. She had six horses to tack up. And then of course there were the five children, who weren't due to be collected until the evening, and not all of the mothers were at home, I think. So Kit went to telephone their homes while Val waited out here to send the children on their usual ride."

Hobden dotted a final note. "And as you haven't been here for so long, Miss Aubrey, it's no use asking you if you noticed anything unusual this morning."

"I've never been *here* at all," Diana pointed out. "When Val was teaching me to ride, she hadn't a school, only a couple of ponies for her and Caspar. I knew Mrs. Cullen by sight when Benjamin was a baby. There was nothing unusual about Val, that's all I know. She hadn't changed a bit."

Kit Cullen had even less to tell him. No, she had not gone into any part of the stables before Valentine's arrival; she had quite enough to look after with her children, her house, and her shop. Yes, of course she and Valentine helped one another out when necessary, but when things were running normally that was not necessary, and, yes, things had appeared to be running quite normally this morning.

"In spite of Jill's absence, Mrs. Cullen?"

"It didn't strike me that she was absent. The girls knew their jobs and got on with them. So did I."

With admirable brevity she explained the business relationship between Valentine and herself. "She rents my yard and big stable and has my children's two ponies at half-livery, which gives her the use of them when they're spare. We keep our yards separate, for practical reasons, stable business in at the stable gate, shop at the farm gate. I'd lose custom if my entrance was cluttered up with ponies and collecting parents. Even when they mount by the big stable they take care to keep to their own side."

"And last evening, ma'am?"

"What about it?"

"The dead girl came here."

"No she didn't. She came to the stables. I neither saw nor heard her."

Hobden took the edge off her sharpness by observing mildly, "I imagine that wouldn't be possible if you were in the house."

"You're quite right, it isn't. The big stable shields us. Even if the stable light's on you can only see a faint glow from here."

"Can you hear anything?"

"From the yard, yes, but not very clearly. From inside the small stable, no. In any case it was my baking evening and I had the radio on."

"So the evening with you was just normal? And that would be from what time?"

Kit's leathery little face did not change. "From about six-thirty when Valentine put the keys through the window and called that she was going."

There was a delay before Jonty Barton could be interviewed, because her parents had not arrived. Hobden went into the stable yard and spoke to Cheal.

"All okay, sir, ambulance away and photographer just finishing. Not a hope of dabs; weapon pitted with rust; even the bolts on the shed too rough."

"Surgeon confirms the weapon?"

"No doubt of it, he says. It had been wired to hang, but the wire was broken, quite recently. Held by one end. First blow killed her, he thinks; hard, but not as hard as the others, which he called mad terror. Someone not much taller—she was five-six—and right-handed."

"Clear enough pattern," Hobden grunted.

"Argument turns into quarrel, girl sweeps past him, he hits out with whatever's to hand— Do we know where the horseshoe came from, by the way?"

Hobden made a note.

"Girl falls, blood everywhere, he gets frightened and hits with all he's got."

"He?"

"Fairly strong, according to the doc."

"Um. Riding: develops the muscles," said Hobden. "No; think I agree, Bert: he. Boy-friend type of quarrel. Got him in here, probably." He showed him Valentine's address book.

Cheal was impressed. "Someone making things easy for us. Not that it's going to be necessary, if you ask me."

"Yes?"

"Blood-stained clothes. Jeans and trainers and a T-shirt, most like. If there wasn't a garden bonfire for us to spot, a bundle shoved into a ditch; and a mum to notice they're missing."

Hobden made a sour face. "Don't know which is the worse—family knows and won't tell, family knows and will tell."

Cheal, who had not arrived at such scruples, knew his chief better than not to acquiesce. A Land-Rover turned in at the yard, and Jonty came slowly from the big stable and was enveloped by the embraces of a little roundabout woman and two six-foot young men. "What's the betting that little Miss Jonty there can make a very good guess at the murderer?"

Little Miss Jonty sat in front of them with her fierce little mother at her elbow, two brothers at the ready, and a father said to be on the way. They were immensely proud of her, listening with admiration to her replies, which were considered and open and ready. The lids under her wide bee-stung brows were shiny and reddened, but her main air was of bewilderment. In her childish face the lips lifted so naturally into the round cheeks that even serious she seemed to wear a faint, sometimes ironic, smile. She began carefully at half past six on Thursday evening. She and Jill had taken four out-grazers to Melcotts and walked back with the bridles to Hole Cottage. They had showered and changed for the disco and had supper. No, not with Valentine, who was home by that time, but upstairs because they were doing their hair. Valentine had driven them to the Youth Club just after seven-thirty, where John had met them. They had not gone in for twenty minutes or so, because there was a row of powerful motor bicycles parked outside and they suspected there was going to be trouble. At last someone who had been in came out and reported that "the rough crowd up from the coast" were there and were bound to spoil the evening; so Fiona, whom they had met, invited them to her house, and they had gone there in John's car. No, she hadn't expected that Jill would want to spend the evening with Fiona, but they had to go with John because they had promised Val. Specially?—not really, she supposed, but it was understood that they played fair about transport.

"That sounds a promise it's not easy to keep," Hobden prompted.

Jonty looked blank, and then faintly smiled. "No, we do keep it. It's a bore sometimes, but no use in fiddling. You'd only get stuck miles away and have to ring up to be fetched. And Val'd be a terror if we did that."

"You've discovered that, then."

"Not us. We once got stuck very late when someone didn't turn up, and she tore him into little pieces."

Surprised that Jill went home?—not really; Fiona was very wet and Jill couldn't stand that. "Me?—well, I stayed with John because we're together, and Fiona's records are all right." No, she hadn't seen Jill when she came in, and she hadn't heard her; her bedroom door had been closed. But, blinking, she asked, "What shoes has—had—has she got on?"

Hobden turned to his notes. Cheal said, "Flat-heeled strap sandals in red, miss. Looked a bit funny with that smart party get-up."

"Oh, then she'd gone before I got back," Jonty said composedly. "She kept that pair in the kitchen cupboard, and I was tidying before I went to bed and saw they weren't there."

"And that would be—?"

"Well, I got in about twenty to eleven."

"Was that late for her to be out?"

Jonty considered slowly. "Not really. It was a nice night, and not absolutely dark; you didn't need a torch. Val says to be in by eleven generally, but we're always popping in and out."

"Would you have expected her to come to the stables?"

"No," Jonty said at once. "No reason."

"If she wanted to meet someone?"

"Someone?" She looked blank again.

"A boy-friend?"

She still looked blank. "Everyone came to the house. Val didn't mind."

"If she wanted to meet him in se—alone?"

"Oh, Jill never bothered about that."

"Now, Miss Jonty," said Hobden, tailoring his words to her mother, "I don't mean anything wrong. But when you've got a new boy-friend you don't want anyone else around, do you?"

"Jill never slept with her boy-friends," Jonty said disarmingly, while her mother bounced gently on her chair. "She was too bored with them all."

"If they'd gone for a stroll, then, and found themselves by the stables?"

"She wouldn't have disturbed the blue-eyed cream."

"But she did disturb him, my dear. No guesses why?"

Jonty could not even frown properly; her bee-stung brows had not yet developed the wrinkles. They drew into bumps as she said directly, "No guesses at all. I've been thinking about it. It was silly. Jill doesn't do silly things."

"I'm not sure that I know what you mean by silly, my dear."

Jonty looked gently baffled; it was a minute or two before he realized that what was baffling her was the problem of making him understand her. "Well—rushing off into the night, you know. Like rushing upstairs and banging your door. Noticeable sort of things."

"Spectacular," said her mother, patting her hand.

"Yes, mum. When people do that sort of thing, they only want to be noticed. Jill never did that."

Hobden considered her with interest. "She didn't want to be noticeable? Now I'd got quite a different idea of her, from her family circumstances."

"Oh, them," Jonty said tolerantly. "They were awful to her. Never even came to see her ride at shows, and she kept all her cups and rosettes at Val's. She hadn't wanted *them* to notice her for years. And everyone knew her here; she was spectacular."

"That's very perceptive of you, my dear. So, since she did come here to the stables, there must have been some special reason. Now I know you've said you don't know that reason, but try making a guess. What sort of reason would it have to be?"

"Oh, something wrong with the horses," said Jonty, stating the obvious.

"Such as?"

"Well, nothing that fits. If they'd broken out; but they can't break out of the home field with Kit's wiring. Or if one of them was down; but they're all in good nick."

"And if it had been either of those, wouldn't it have been Mrs. Cullen who would discover it first, and ring you?"

"Not in the small stable; she wouldn't go in after Val had left."

"Suppose one of the horses had broken out on the other side of the field. That would bring it—let's see—on to the common, or into the strip of woodland and then the back gardens of Hollow Cross. No, suppose someone had come to your door and told Jill he'd seen them straying."

"Yes, she'd go then, if she believed it. But not without telling Val."

"Suspicious movements around the stables? No, she'd have rung Mrs. Cullen. Well," said Hobden, abandoning this point, "tell me, have you seen an old horseshoe round the stable lately?"

"Yes, old Blossom's. That was the last shire they had here. Ben Cullen kept her after they went over to tractors. It used to hang on the rafter in the small stable, but the wire broke the other week and no one had got round to hanging it again. What was—did that—?"

"Now, no need to trouble your head," said her mother, who had plainly had a word with Kit, and Hobden took the hint and went straight on.

"Tell me what kind of girl Jill was. Many friends, for instance?"

"Boy-friends?"

"If you like."

"Well, if you asked the lads, they'd say every one of them—now she's not here to tell them off. If you'd asked her, she'd have said no one."

"Lads?"

"The stable-lads. That's what we call all the helpers: girls as well, actually. Oh, didn't Val explain that? Well, we need a lot of help in our busy times, and there are a dozen or so volunteers. Not the young ones, twelve and thirteen; they're just general help. The lads have to be good riders, and they're all fifteen or sixteen or more. The two best are girls, Margaret Clarke and Lucy Kinsella; they really make the effort. The boys won't; they just stroll down when they haven't anything better to do."

"They live locally?" Hobden interrupted.

"Not Margaret; she's a good ten miles away, but her mum has that dress-shop in the High Street and can give her transport. Lucy's two miles away, but she can bike. All the boys come from Hollow Cross."

"And who are they?"

Jonty considered, and at last brought out the list Hobden had been hoping for.

"There's Paul Crossly. His father used to have the Swan at Yearly."

"He left eighteen months ago."

"Yes, but they've only gone twenty miles away, and Paul visits his gran a lot. He's smooth, just like his dad, who tried to turn the Swan into a high-class noshery and just spoilt a good local, but he's not bad otherwise, and the best rider of the lot. And there's Kevin Higgins. I expect you know the Higginses."

Hobden did. Steve Higgins had a few sour acres, where he did precious little farming but a great deal of scrap-dealing, all of it dubious.

"He went right through school labelled non-exam, and everyone knows he can add four columns of figures in his head and add V.A.T. and forty per cent mark-up without a blink. Be a scrap millionaire by the time he's twenty, probably. Colin Hewens always tagged after him because he thought he was wonderful, the poor oaf. Both of them have left school now, and of course Colin's got no job. He's a bit heavy-handed as a rider, but at least he does know it's a horse he's on and not a motor bike. Jill stood him for that, and probably because everyone else said he was thick."

"What exactly do you mean by *stood him?*"

"Not a lot," Jonty said frankly. "He was too slow to ask her out, but I know they were together a couple of evenings. We always go out in a bunch because of the transport, so they probably got together when Jill ditched someone else. She was rather a ditcher. Kevin and Paul of course asked her out properly, but it didn't do them any more good."

"And is that all?"

"Oh, no," Jonty said obligingly. "There was Chris, Chris Tidy from up the road, son of the man with the apple trees at the corner, the one they call Monkey because he's such a contortionist. He was famous for that at school, and he came swaggering down here thinking he'd do better than anyone else, but actually he wasn't as good as Colin; his balance was fantastic, but it never occurred to him that a horse has balance too. And there was poor little Mark—that's Mark Pollard from that converted farm beyond the Cross; you wouldn't think it, but he's nearly sixteen too. He can't help being nervous—people are born like that and he works hard at it, but Jill had no time for him. Well, I don't believe he ever thought she would have; he was just too willing to be a doormat. That's all I can think of now. Gary Thing—no, he left at Easter; anyway he came pretending he could ride just to impress Jill, and she put him up on Ebony and watched Eb wipe him off."

"They are all what you call the stable-lads?"

"Uh-huh. Not Gary, scrub Gary. Mark sort of, because he's sensible and tries hard, even if he's not much of a rider."

"Didn't Jill have any boy-friend who wasn't a rider?"

Jonty reflected. "Not really. She wouldn't have been interested in anyone who wasn't a rider. And it was only riders who saw her to admire her."

"Are your boy-friends riders, Miss Jonty?"

Jonty broke into a chuckle. "John thinks horses are barbarous."

"Then why—"

Mrs. Barton broke in reprovingly, "John's a very nice boy and his family are friends of ours. Our Jonty may be good with horses but she do have other things in her head as well."

"You mean that Jill didn't?"

They looked at Jonty, who smiled her faint bewildered smile. "Little Mark once said there were only two boy-friends who would have been good enough for Jill."

Hobden was trying to remember the names of current show-jumpers when Jonty finished, "The Darley Arab and the Godolphin Barb."

CHAPTER 3

"I suppose this is lunch," Kit said tiredly as she dumped the plates on the kitchen table, "but it could be supper or tomorrow's breakfast for all I know."

Diana murmured politely, "It's very kind of you," and slid into her place.

Valentine looked questioningly at the extra two covers. "Benjamin and Bridie: have we to be careful of what we say?"

"No. They've got to know," Kit said briefly.

"Know what?" Bridie lisped sweetly, appearing at once.

"Listening!" Kit snapped.

"Yes, but I couldn't hear. What has happened to poor Jill?"

"She's dead," said Benjamin, coming moodily in.

"Yes, I know, but how?"

Kit breathed stormily. "Now look. I won't have you two hanging around guessing. It's not nice, but you'll hear about it somehow, so get it over now. Someone knocked Jill on the head last night in the small stable and she died of it. We don't know yet who did it, but whoever it was is on the run from the police, so don't get any horrors or I shall send you off to your grandmother's."

"You can't do that!" said Benjamin. "I have to school Florian every day."

"Then be sensible. And, just for the record, did either of you hear anything unusual last night?"

"We were asleep," said Bridie sadly.

"Will there be an inquest and all that jazz?" Benjamin enquired suspiciously.

"Yes, but not until Monday because of the week-end. And the funeral—Val, we'll have to stay closed until the day after that, don't you think?"

"I will," said Valentine, who was eating quickly. "You needn't. You'd better not. Jill's parents are on some coach trip in France; Hobden was saying it might be as long as a week."

Kit blanched; a week's closing meant the loss of stock carefully brought on. "That would make a hole. But to serve in the shop, knowing that everyone was dying to ask me—and most of them probably would be asking me—"

Diana said shyly, "Couldn't I see to the shop for you? No one seems to remember me here."

"That's very good of you," said Kit, showing her astonishment rather too plainly. "Then I could help Val with the stable-work. You won't get the lads, Val. Or if you do you'll have to send them away smartish."

Valentine nodded in comprehension. "Why?" Benjamin demanded.

"Because they'll only have come out of ghoulish curiosity."

Benjamin looked livelier; he was going to find himself in a privileged position. "We'll help in the stable," he decided generously. "Can I have some apple pie now?"

Valentine refused apple pie. "Got to get back."

"Why?" Kit asked ominously, and fixed her with a very nasty eye.

Valentine nodded to the eye and the tone. "But the police want to see Jill's room. And then I suppose I must pack her things for her parents to collect."

"That won't be yet."

"I want it done."

"Where's Jonty?" Bridie asked, her covetous look on the pie Valentine had refused.

"Gone home with her family."

"Well, what about her share of the stable-work?"

"It'll have to be done, that's all."

Diana offered shyly, "They surely won't want her to come back?"

No one seemed to have thought of this. Even Valentine looked uncertain.

Bridie said placidly, "That won't matter. Jonty will come."

Kit went to the door with Valentine, saying, "You'll be here for supper?" Her face was threatening.

"Yes," Valentine said at once; "yes, I'll be here for supper."

In the kitchen of Hole Cottage, the coffee-pot, left on for Jill, was desolately brewing still. On the draining board two mugs stood upside down; on the table still lay a clean mug and plate beside the toaster. Hobden inspected the telephone pad in the hall, with its two last messages in Jill's hand.

"Could either of these calls have suggested a walk to the stables?" he suggested.

Valentine shook her head. "Look up these families in my address book. Both at a distance, both girls of eleven and twelve."

"Could she have made a call herself?"

"Well, try."

Hobden went into the sitting-room with the door closed and the television switched on. The bell was clearly audible.

"Anyway," Valentine added with a little impatience, "anyone could have come to the back door, and I wouldn't have heard that; people round here don't knock, they open the door and shout. My hedges are too high for anything to be seen from the lane, but someone might have seen her going out or someone else coming in."

Hobden made a wry face. "Towards the stables? You're the last house on this side; not many people about here at that time of night. Might be a chance. Now upstairs if I may, ma'am."

Upstairs were three small bedrooms and the bathroom. The bathroom, with wet towels all over it, showed that someone had had a bath that morning. Valentine's room was neat; Jonty's had the bed nominally made and her last-night's party dress sprawled over the chair. It was thoroughly Jonty's; there were piles of magazines, a radio, photographs of horses and her family stuck over the walls.

Jill's was quite different. The bed was smooth, the make-up on the dressing-table tidily ranged. On the shelf over the small cottage fireplace was a row of silver cups, well polished, and above them a home-made board covered with rosettes. The wardrobe held several pairs of worn jeans, a couple of summer dresses, a pair of old jodhpurs, and, carefully hung and covered, a pair of new jodhpurs and a black show-jacket. On the wall opposite the bed, not carelessly pinned like Jonty's but painstakingly backed with cardboard and covered with polythene, was the blown-up photograph of a pale horse.

"There is not one single thing in here," said Valentine after a time, "that she hadn't bought or won herself, or that Jonty or I hadn't given her." She shook off her anger by going to look more closely at the blown-up photograph. "I didn't know she'd got that already. Mark must have done it quickly for her."

"Mark?"

"He gave her a small print, and offered to make an enlargement. It's good, isn't it?"

It was taken from a curious angle, the horse looking sombrely down at the camera as if from a high place. The light had been obliquely behind it, so that it dazzled through the forelock but caught the fan of the eyelashes and threw a queer light into the eyeballs. There was a china-blue centre to this queer gleam, and Hobden said, "Ah—the horse you call the blue-eyed cream, ma'am?"

"Yes," said Valentine with her eyes fast on it. "The one in the small stable. She—no, silly to say she loved that horse. She could handle him when no one else could, let's say. I hadn't found a name for him; none of them sounded quite right; but she had some secret name, though I can't remember that I ever heard it properly. . . . Do you like that photo, Mr. Hobden?"

Hobden considered it. "It's very striking. And a clever piece of work."

"Oh, clever, yes; nice to think that poor little Mark can do something. Why do I dislike it so intensely, then? It seems to remind me of something horrible, and a very long time ago. . . . Well. If you find masculine things around, they belong to my son. The girls double up—*doubled* up—when he came down. Can I go and clean the downstairs rooms that you've seen? I'm not used to hanging around the house at this time of day."

"I'd rather you left them until we've had a closer look, ma'am. My men will be here directly."

Furious, Valentine went out and summer-pruned her apple trees, refusing to look at whoever came and went. When they had permitted her her house again, she returned to Jill's room. The dirty clothes went into the washing machine. Jill had never had a suitcase, her belongings having arrived in a series of plastic bags. Finding one of her own, Valentine methodically packed in everything but the riding clothes, which went into Jonty's room; hung out the washed clothes, stripped the bed, cleaned the room, ironed the dry clothes and put them on top of the suitcase, and drew the curtains over the window and put the suitcase at the back of her own wardrobe.

That left only the photograph of the blue-eyed cream on the wall. It was too big to put safely anywhere else, and in the end she left it there and closed the bedroom door. She did not like it, but she had the idea that it reminded her of something important; and she did not want to be reminded of anything just now.

In the summer evenings Kit sat by the long window in the kitchen, doing her booking, doing her mending, doing her ironing; it was odd and uneasy to see her with her hands empty on her lap.

"About time you explained," she said.

"First chance I've had," Valentine said defensively.

"I hold it against you, I warn you. You manoeuvred me into concealing evidence, and vital evidence at that. We could be in serious trouble for that."

"I didn't manoeuvre you. You could have spoken up for yourself."

"When they'd talked to you first and I knew you hadn't spoken up?"

"It was still your own doing and not mine; and we both know why."

"You can talk your way out of anything," Kit said with a flash of temper, "but it doesn't alter the fact."

"All right," said Valentine, subsiding, "let's talk about the fact. Can't we even have some coffee?"

Kit got up with a sigh and filled the pot. "Just what idiocy came over you, for heaven's sake? That silly trick of pretending that Gingerbread was lame, when you'd ridden him up and it was obvious he was all right!"

"I can be wrong. You think of anything better when you have about two seconds to spare. I could hear you. Any moment you were going to let out that I never leave the stables without putting Dandy on guard."

"So you shut me up," said Kit tiredly.

"Here," said Valentine. She brought out half a bottle of whisky. "Captain's coffee: you'll feel better when you've had some. Okay, I admit I sprang this on you, but you had plenty of time before Hobden saw you, and you can look after yourself. Come on; you managed to answer him without an actual lie, didn't you?"

"Oh, of course I did; that was easy enough. But it won't *last*, you fool. He'll be back on the doorstep tomorrow, and then what are we going to do?"

"One thing at a time." Valentine poured two mugs and laced them generously. "Drink up and you'll feel less doom-laden. What we are considering first is what *you* are going to do. That's easy too. You're going to be blankly ignorant. The stables are mine and you don't interfere with my arrangements. Dandy's my guard dog by night, and whether I use him to guard my stables or my house is my affair and not yours. Don't *worry*, Kit."

"And what about you?"

"That's my funeral." Valentine shut her mouth on the words, and Kit knew her too well to press the point.

"Then be warned. I have Benjamin and Bridie to think of, and if I have to I shall dump you. But that point being settled—yes?"

"Of course."

"Then will you kindly tell me what the *hell* you think you're doing?"

"I can't be sure, can I?" said Valentine mildly, "but I hope I'm stopping the police discovering who killed Jill."

Kit looked at her for some time, speechless. At last she said, "Do you know who killed her?"

"No. Do you?"

"My God, *no.*"

"But since Dandy was on guard we have a short list to choose from, don't we? Dandy would have let in only those who had the right to come and go. In fact it's the stable-lads, isn't it? He did learn to know some of the liveries who rode a lot, but they've left now. It has to be Kevin, Colin, Chris, Paul, Lucy, or Margaret. Oh, or I suppose Mark."

Going through the list in her head, Kit went bluish-pale. "*The lads*: they've been here all this time; talking to us; riding with us. . . . Val, not Margaret or Lucy, I think. Not because they're girls. Transport."

"Yes. I hadn't much thought of them anyway; too level-headed both."

"But the others—you couldn't bring yourself to shop any of them."

"Nor could you, could you?"

"I hadn't had time to think."

"You have now. So?"

"I don't like the idea," Kit said stoutly, "but I like much less Jill dead."

"Christ, do you think I like it?" Valentine got up with a violent movement and calmed herself by taking a packet of cigarettes from her pocket. "That's the end of my stopping smoking," she remarked flippantly. "Roll on the day when I can start stopping again." She lit her cigarette and took a long pull on it. "Look, let's think a bit about what happened last night. Someone came to my kitchen door and spoke to Jill; and something he said decided her to go with him."

"Why couldn't he have met her on the way home from Fiona's?"

"A feeling I have. Jill wasn't one to hide her moods, and when she came in to see me I don't believe she had anything on her mind."

"Yes," Kit agreed doubtfully. "But what did he say that decided her?"

"We don't know and probably never will. Why should we? I get along with the girls and the lads as well as most, and, more than that, I hear them talking among themselves rather more than most; and I don't understand a tenth of what goes on. They've got their own world and we're not included, any more than they are included in our world. He was just a poor stupid boy all full of calf-love for Jill, and Jill didn't care a damn for him and was quite ready to make that clear."

"She always was," Kit said sighing. "She could be incredibly wounding. But, Val, however wounded, to kill like *that*—"

"Oh no, no, *no*. Kit, you don't see it! It was only the first blow that was delivered in anger, don't you understand? And even that was a mistake—because the old horseshoe was to his hand. *And* because it was delivered when Jill was walking past him, and so caught her on the worst possible spot, the temple. If he had done what was in his mind to do, he would have given her a black eye— and most likely got one himself in return. But when he saw what he had done, the rest would have been in sheer terror."

Kit thought about it, shivered, and reluctantly nodded.

"Another point," Valentine added. "I told Hobden this, but there was only my word to go on and I don't know if he took much notice. You remember that I was creosoting the yard fence just before I left last night? With that old plastic mack over my clothes? When I'd done I dropped it on the pile of mucking-out clothes in the small stable. This morning it was still there, lying just the way I'd left it but covered with splashes of blood. The murderer must have been badly splashed too, but he hadn't thought to take anything from the pile to save his clothes. Which he would have done if he'd planned it, wouldn't he?"

Interested in spite of herself, Kit objected, "But what about those splashed clothes—how would he get rid of them? And he had to get home—didn't anyone see him?"

"Or see Jill and him coming here?" Valentine achieved a genuine laugh. "Lovey, it's a whole day since it was discovered. If anyone in the neighbourhood had seen anything, is there a soul in Hollow Cross who wouldn't have heard of it by now? No, it's a lonely road from my place to yours. And as for his getting home, they all have their private gaps and short cuts and illegal footpaths. The clothes, though—yes, he'd have to think about that. There are bonfires; kitchen stoves are lit in summer if they provide the hot water. There will be a pair of jeans missing, and perhaps some mother will notice that. Perhaps not, though. When Caspar was sixteen I washed what was put for me."

Kit was no longer listening; she was out of the room at a stifled noise from upstairs. Valentine made more coffee, and presently Kit returned with her sandy brows tightened with worry.

"Bridie. I thought she'd stopped having nightmares. She's gone off again."

"About Jill?"

"General upset, I think. She made me look out of the window and swear I could see Cupid."

The little Exmoor was Bridie's own pony. "Why Cupid? There's never anything wrong with him."

"I think she'd been dreaming he was stolen. More coffee?—how many pints have we got through today, I wonder. Where were we?"

"Well, I think you'd stopped swearing at me."

"More fool me if I had. Val, do you seriously want this boy to be let go?"

"If I had what I seriously wanted, as you put it, this boy probably would never have been born. As he was, the least harmful thing I can think of now is for him to be let go. Do you want to see him shut up for ten years, learning how to be the accomplished criminal he isn't yet? And if you're thinking that he ought to be punished for killing Jill—if your likings incline that way—oh, Kit, don't worry! He's had twenty hours of it already. Do you think he isn't regretting, like us, that he was ever born?"

After a time Kit said only, "The children have nothing clean for tomorrow," and got out her ironing-board. Valentine lifted down the basket of washing and started sorting it.

"What's Diana like?" Kit asked presently. "Can she manage the shop?"

"Too rich and too pretty all her life, but that's not her fault. She'll give the wrong change half a dozen times and make it up from her own purse, which she can well afford so let her, and she'll be so decorative and beautifully mannered that you won't lose."

"You will, though."

Valentine acknowledged this with a downward twist of her lips. With winter feed bills to be met throughout the lean months, the loss of a week's fees was a serious matter.

"Any horse ready to sell on?"

"There's the blue-eyed cream."

"He's not schooled."

"He's rideable. He'd make more if I could afford to

wait, but he's so handsome he'd go to the right buyer any time now."

Kit put down her iron and said with surprising decision, "No. Don't let's sell Jill's horse the moment Jill's gone. Let's be sentimental and try to keep him. Let Jonty take him over and make something out of him."

"Perhaps Jonty will tell us what his name is. I must be going, Kit. Asleep on my feet."

"Thanks for the whisky," Kit said grudgingly. "And as for Jill's murderer, well, we don't agree, and I shall tell the truth if I'm asked. And I think you'll change your mind soon and tell it yourself without being asked."

"Oh? At any particular time?"

"Yes. The first time one of the lads strolls in at the gate and you realize you may be riding with a murderer."

Valentine broke into a soft laugh. "Oh, Kit—you haven't seen it yet. You don't think he'll face this place again? Which he will be quite safe in doing. Remember the time of year?"

"The school holidays," said Kit, struck.

"And the end of the school year. And the stable-lads are all sixteen. Do we ever see the sixteen-year-olds after July? They go on holiday, they get jobs, they go on the dole, they go away to college, and then they find they've grown up and it's beneath their dignity to shovel muck for women. We've seen the last of them, Kit; leave them be."

CHAPTER 4

By Saturday evening Hobden and Cheal had developed opposing theories about the Stumbletts murder.

They had opposing theories about the detection of crime. Hobden had been a boy in one of the villages, in the days when efficient crime-prevention was the sight of the local copper talking to your dad, and his view was that detection was no more than common sense backing up some obvious enquiries. Cheal favoured scientific detection and logical methods of analysis. He put everything on to punched cards, whose codes he refined until no one else understood them, and prided himself on being able to turn up every irrelevant detail within seconds. Hobden sincerely admired his beautiful paperwork, and was glad to have someone checking the bits that did not matter.

By Saturday evening most of the obvious work had been done. There were no pleasant surprises, no unexpected pieces of good luck. No one had seen Jill on Thursday night. A great many people along Church Lane and in the Hollow Cross area had seen girls in party dress; but half the girls in the neighbourhood had been straggling

home from the disco, and by an unlucky chance the other
half had been at a birthday party in Church Lane. There
were always people outside on a fair evening in Hollow
Cross, on the bench outside the pub, in their back gardens, working on their cars on the kerb. Hole Lane, on
the other hand, was narrow, overgrown, and lonely; if you
lived in Hole Lane and wanted conversation, you walked
up to the Cross. No one had seen Jill arrive or leave; no
one had seen John bring Jonty home; no one had even
seen Valentine come home.

With some care, they had interviewed the stable-lads.

The two girls, Margaret and Lucy, were easy, being together ("As we might have guessed," Hobden grunted),
and having been together talking about Jill ever since the
news of her death. They were what Cheal called O-level,
if not A-level, types: equally ready to be serious and re-
sponsible or to relax into gossip. It quite plainly had never
entered either head that they could be suspected of anything.

Lucy, a brown-skinned black-eyed chuckler, had been
with a boy-friend to the disco.

"Well, being there early we'd paid, and we wanted our
money's worth, didn't we? Ken's father's one of the
helpers there, so he knows his way about, and when it got
rough we found the key of the upstairs room and nipped
up and played table tennis all the evening. Margaret
wasn't there."

"Couldn't get transport," Margaret said with reserve.
She was a very blond, slightly awkward girl with the
faintly priggish look of the woman who has made up her
mind that she is unattractive. Hobden suspected that it
was not transport but a boy-friend that had not been
available.

"Did you see Jill at all?"

"In that ruck? Mr. Hobden, you don't know what the place is *like* on a disco evening."

"I do," Cheal said grinning. "Been there often when I was in the uniformed branch. Everyone hangs about outside at first."

"Oh, I thought you meant to talk to. We spotted Val's old van leaving, and then we saw the whole crowd of them miles from the door."

"There were only three of them."

"There were about twenty when I saw them."

"Can you remember the others?" said Hobden, prudently reducing the numbers by a quarter.

Lucy rolled her handsome eyes to indicate impossibility, but produced a very fair reply. "They were probably asking what it was like inside, so they'd talk to anyone they knew. The only one I can really be sure of was Paul Crossly; I saw him talking to John. Paul always knows the inside stories of things like discos."

"Christidy was going, I think," said Margaret.

"Who's that?"

"Tiddy Chris: Christopher Tidy. That little squinched-up boy who lives just by the Cross."

"He fancies you," Lucy accused her. "I bet he asked you to go with him."

"And I told him where he could go without me," said Margaret wrathfully. Resigned to plainness, she still retained her pride.

"Well, I don't know if he did go; I never saw him."

"Were either of you at Stumbletts on Thursday?"

"Oh, yes; both of us, all day. We're always there in the holidays. They can't manage with only the grooms and Val on a heavy day, and no one can rely on the boys. They only turn up when they've nothing better to do."

"Anyway," Margaret added, "it's the only way of getting enough riding. If I had to pay for my riding I'd get an hour a week."

"Ten minutes, me," sighed Lucy, her bright black eyes inviting their sympathy.

"Did you notice anything out of the way then?"

"Do you think we haven't gone *over* and *over* it?" Lucy demanded.

"Four rides," Margaret said quietly, "usual number of riders, no strangers. One of them schooling, the other three the usual hack."

"No one quarrelled, no one came off—"

"Where is the usual hack?" Hobden interrupted.

"Out by the back gate, over the common, and then along the old road—you know that?"

Cheal nodded. The main road to the coast had been straightened some years before to avoid the narrow streets of the town, and the old road, now blocked off, had fallen into disuse except by walkers, running in a broad embanked curve for five miles along one side of the common. "A good place for riding."

"Great, so long as you get to know the pot-holes. We always go as far as Hugletts Bridge, where the Hugletts farm road goes underneath; that's thirty-five minutes out and twenty-five back, so it's just right for an hour's ride."

"I was riding herd on all three," Lucy said, "and Jill was with me, and she was just as usual."

"What did you talk about?"

"We didn't. That's Jill being just as usual. Well, a few remarks about the ride."

"And what about in-between?"

"There isn't any in-between when you have to dismount a ride, perhaps change some horses, and mount the next. Lunch-time we all ate our sandwiches in the yard. At the end of the day Jill and Jonty took the only out-grazers, so Margaret and I walked down Hollow Lane until her mum picked us up. Only thing I noticed about Jill was that she didn't bite anybody's head off for once."

"That's not fair," said Margaret. "She didn't bully."

"Miss Lucy didn't get on with her, then?"

"Oh, I got *on* with her. I just stood up to her now and again, for the good of her soul."

"I was sorry for her," Margaret said surprisingly. "I know she was a fearful bitch at times, but only when someone was being stupid. And sometimes she was rather splendid."

"Only when she was on a horse, alas," said Lucy. "And the human condition demands just a little bit more than that."

With the boys they drew a complete blank, which perhaps they should have expected.

There were no Pollards at Snaggs Farm, which these days was all raked gravel and diamond-smooth weatherboarding; only a suspicious woman who said she was the housekeeper. Mr. Pollard was abroad on business, Mrs. Pollard was staying with friends, and Mark had gone to see his cousin in Devon. Since when?—ten-thirty on Friday they had called to collect him.

Sighing, Hobden began a preamble about Mark's possibly being a witness to a sad affair in the neighbourhood—

"I'd call it a disgraceful affair. But if people will live near council estates— As for Mark being witness to anything, of course he wasn't. Thursday evening he was in all the time from half past six till his bedtime. I took him a tray of supper myself in that room they've let him fix up for messing about with his photographs."

She nodded towards the room. It was in a converted barn, and from the upper window a staircase led to the ground.

"And after supper?"

"He's big enough to see himself into bed. I'm not paid as a nursemaid."

At Oakley Farm Mrs. Higgins was drinking tea and reading the *Sun*. She was in heelless slippers and a sagging dress, and in the yard sad gummy-eyed kittens slept on old newspapers and muddy wisps of feathers around the wheels of a very new car.

Kevin was away on business, she said.

"Business—Kevin?"

"He's gone in with his dad now he's done with school. He's a good boy, that one, and ought to do as well as his dad. They've gone up to London on a deal."

"You know where they're staying?"

"Oh, they'll put up somewhere if they stay. Or maybe with friends."

Cheal asked, "I suppose they didn't take Kevin's mate with them by any chance—young Colin Hewens?"

"Oh, you know Colin? Well, it was a kindness, wasn't it? He's got no job, and he's a good strong boy, and my Jack isn't one to grudge a boy his wage. Very grateful young Colin was, to give him his due, because he isn't the kind to make a business man like our Kevin."

"So when we next try to nail Jack Higgins on a stolen load, he'll have Colin to take the rap," Cheal said bitterly as they came away. "He should have stayed shovelling muck for Mrs. Brooke. Ask me, sir, we aren't going to get anywhere with any of them. Nice weather, summer holiday: hopeless."

It was; at their remaining call, a house at the corner of the Hollow Cross estate, a neighbour looked out to say, "No good knocking, they're away."

"Know where, missus?"

"Fishing. Mad on it both of them, get away whenever they can. Went this morning."

"Hang on," said Cheal as Hobden was turning away. "Mr. Tidy—not Fred Tidy the sweet-pea man?"

"That's him. Everyone knows him."

"Well, well," said Cheal as they got back into the car. "If there was ever a man my old man hated it was Fred Tidy. Beat him on sweet peas every single year at all the flower shows. Thought the name rang a bell."

"What's he like?"

"Oh, nice chap. Decorator, I think—no, carpenter; always worked for Cotter's. Biggish family; three girls, I think, all married years ago and gone away and Chris was the last by several years. Bit of discreet doubt about him once; wife went a bit wild and eventually moved out, but Fred thinks the world of him. Let's see: if he's sixteen or so I'd just have left secondary school as he was starting. Yes, it's coming back—gymnast little Miss Jonty said he was? Didn't get him at once because no one ever used his given name; he was always Titch Tidy. Pride of the school for a bit, got his B.A.G.A. badges without even trying, everyone saying they'd got an Olympic champ here. Silly, of course; they don't have the training for that sort of standard around here, even if he had been that good; never even made county standard when it came to it."

"Monkey, she said they called him."

"They would. All legs and arms, one of those tremendously arched backs, and a real monkey face, little slit eyes and a long thin grin. I remember Fred's fishing too. Used to come home with the back of his van full and smelling to high heaven, and go round everyone with damp newspaper parcels. Walk down the road and smell fish frying in every kitchen, and they'd say that Fred was home again."

"Then we can continue our investigations when we smell fish," said Hobden, whom the morning had reduced to a rare bad temper. "No, I don't want them rounded up and pulled in, any of them. Gently has to do it in this case."

It was when these routine enquiries had been laboriously gone through that Cheal developed his counter-theory. He brought it to Hobden with a shy smile and a determination to make the dramatic most of it, which Hobden, who had not recovered his temper, did not treat kindly.

"Bert, it's getting late and I want to get home and have my dinner at a comfortable hour. If you've got something up your sleeve, out with it sharpish."

"Well, *I* think it's something," said Cheal, wounded, "but of course if you're still set on your boy-friend theory—"

"I said *out* with it."

Cheal opened Valentine's address book. "Checking this as a matter of routine, sir. Mrs. Brooke said she has no liveries who are men, but I thought what about husbands delivering wives, getting into talk with an attractive girl—the old story."

"Medical evidence, Bert. Little Miss Jonty was right; she didn't sleep with them."

"Hadn't seen it then, sir. I'm telling you how I got on to this. Checked the liveries right back to the beginning. And see who I came up with."

He laid it proudly in front of Hobden. Hobden looked at it in frank astonishment.

Mrs. Barbara Cantrell, Corner Oak, Belmanoir Drive. 30. 8½ st. Novice, rode as child. Livery, Sheba, 15hh., chestnut with snip. Added below was: *Brian C., 35, 11 st., experienced*. Printed in a corner over Sheba's name was the single word *SOLD* with a date nearly a year old.

"Interesting?" suggested Cheal, glowing.

Hobden pushed the book aside. "Interesting maybe, but not relevant. You're mixing your worlds, Bert."

"Do we know that, sir?" Cheal persisted.

"Well, tell it as you see it if you must. But do get a move on."

"Haven't had time to do much yet. But Captain Brian Cantrell: we looked into his affairs pretty thoroughly a year or so ago. Another local boy, though not many people realize it and he keeps quiet about it, because old Canty Cantrell wasn't best liked. Whenever there was a nice little bit of land going to be up for sale, somehow he knew of it long before anyone else. Got his planning permissions through too, well before anyone else. He was never actually named in that corruption case, but it was a near thing. Brought his son up a gentleman and died a rich man. Lived like a rich man too, however near to bankruptcy he was. Son grew up thinking money was something you play with, not something you pay the grocer with. Airline pilot now, earns a handsome income but has a divorced wife who puts on the screw with a vengeance. Pretty young second wife—that's our Mrs. Barbara; had a bad time lately, two miscarriages and now a young baby."

"That wasn't what we investigated a year or so ago."

"No; well—" Cheal went a little pink. "My Deb's sister Mandy goes in to clean for her three days a week in their four-bedroom two-bathroom swimming-pool-and-two-acre house. She couldn't give them more than three mornings, so they've got someone else for three more, plus a five-day gardener, plus old Mrs. Dann for the ironing and two schoolgirls for baby-sitting. Of course Mandy talks to Deb, and I've been wondering about him for quite a time. No way at all, it's seemed to me, could he live at that rate and pay off the first wife, even on what an airline pilot earns."

"All right, granted all that; what has it to do with the girl at Stumbletts? The horse was sold a year ago."

"Just about when our gentleman was in the money trouble that so nearly landed him in the soup. Now you look at this." Cheal produced the message-pad from the Stumbletts tack-room. "I went through it on the off-chance. It's mostly things like *So-and-so two-thirty Friday*, but when they finished one page they turned it back and clipped it, so that it must go back a few months. Take a look at this."

Taking up a whole page, a firm square hand had written: *Please tell Val: Took Ebony for an hour—Kit said OK —money in envelope on upper shelf. B.C.C.*

"Brian Charles Cantrell: well," said Hobden, "we can check that. Nothing unusual. If he was an experienced rider—fifteen hands would carry eleven stone—might have ridden his wife's chestnut, might have ridden with her, might have liked an occasional ride after they'd sold their own horse. So what? He was there at a time when Mrs. Brooke wasn't, but he'd seen Mrs. Cullen."

"Let's go back to where we left him. By one of those nasty accidents that befall even the best-organized crime, Pally Kells was caught with a load of cannabis when a lorry ran into his van on the motorway. Died before we could get a word out of him. He was one of Maxie Fist's delivery-men, we know that; but he shouldn't have been running a load then because he worked with Lucky Luckhurst and we'd picked him up that very week. We were ninety per cent sure that instead of Lucky it was our Captain Brian who brought in that load to Pally, he being in just the right place at the right time to fit it in, *and*, as we discovered, deep in debt to his bookmakers, who were the Burrell brothers who do a nice line in finding Maxie useful characters for a little blacking."

"Ninety per cent sure and no material evidence," said Hobden, gently nodding. "And Pally being dead we de-

cided to let it ride and keep an eye on our Captain Brian
in the hope of better things to come."

"Which didn't come. That job was a one-off for him; he
paid his debts and has been a good boy ever since, so far
as we know. Could be he was thoroughly frightened,
could be he didn't like it when he discovered it was drugs
he was carrying. Maxie doesn't like amateurs, anyway."

"Bert," Hobden said patiently, "we still haven't come
to any point. Cantrell is not, repeat not, involved with
Maxie Fist still."

"He's still living at the same rate, though, so he's still in
need of money. What more likely, when he's once safely
delivered a load, than that he'd try again on his own account? Not drugs, most likely; he wouldn't have the contacts for that; but dutiable goods of an easier kind, the
kind you can dispose of without trouble. It would explain
how he gets all the money he's spending."

"We're not trying to explain that."

"It would establish a link," Cheal said stubbornly, "between Stumbletts and the kind of thing people kill for.
Our Captain Brian wouldn't know—amateurs never do
know—but the smuggling game is run by some very nasty
types at the top. Knocking off an odd girl or two would be
nothing to them. Cantrell could come and go at Stumbletts, the note on the pad establishes that. Suppose he'd
been using it for something—don't quite know what—"

"I'll be bound you don't! A place like Hollow Cross,
where everyone knows everyone else's business?"

"Not the business of an occasional rider who arranged
to meet a friend there. And if the girl happened along—or
suspected something and went there purposely? Cantrell's not a killer, I think, but he could easily have got
tied up with someone who was."

Hobden heaved a sigh and sat for some time ruminat-
ing. "Wouldn't lay money on it," he said finally. "Not a

penny. It's a good effort, Bert, very ingenious; but some-how it's not sense. Too many ifs and supposes. But have a go if you like. We're interviewing all Mrs. Brooke's riders, so no harm in including them. There's no date on that note, is there?"

There was not, but in looking for it Cheal found the hidden sheet with the inexplicable message on it.

The Killers are out again.

"Some kids' game," said Hobden.

CHAPTER 5

On the Sunday night the uniformed patrol had a curious encounter, which in due course was reported to Hobden. Driving along Church Lane some way past Hollow Cross, they overtook, rising one by one into the beam of the headlights, a strung-out procession of figures running hard along the grassy verge. Last of them was a boy of fifteen or so, wearing striped pyjama bottoms and struggling with some burden on one arm. Together five yards ahead were two girls, one in an ankle-length skirt and the other in a short and entirely transparent garment. A little ahead of them ran a tall woman in a loose coat, and well ahead and disappearing into the darkness a middle-sized man, normally dressed and running well with his elbows tucked into his sides.

Dickson whistled at the sight of the girls, and Elphick, who was driving, put on speed and cut off the running man against the hedge. He was a stringy middle-aged man who could only double up over the door of the car and flap one hand to indicate that he would explain when he had his breath. The rest of the chase whirled up, and the tall woman said, "Now please—it's all right, there's nothing wrong, but please don't stop us or we shall lose them."

Both men got out of the car, and Dickson said firmly, "Some trouble, madam?" The undressed girl said under her breath something that sounded like, "Bugger *them*," and shot past them with a fine turn of speed. As she went through the headlights it could be seen that she was wearing either very short pyjamas or knickers and a loose shirt. The man straightened up, took a deep breath, said, "You explain, we'll get them," and followed her, plugging along very steadily.

Elphick started to get back into the car, saying, "If you're chasing someone—"

"Most certainly not, you'll only set them off faster," said the tall woman. "Just calm down, all of you." (This was to the police as well as to the remaining runners.) "And, Mark, do please finish dressing." The boy's burden turned out to be a sweater with only one arm in it; he blushed and dived into it. The tall woman turned a powerful smile on Dickson and said, "How nice of you to stop and help us, but if you chase ponies in a car you simply turn them in fright, and then you'll never find them until they've grazed off everyone's lettuce."

"Ponies," said Dickson, enlivened. "We could nip down the twitten, come on them from ahead—"

"There is no need to bother, thank you. Jonty's quite capable of catching them up, and they'll come to her voice. They're both young ponies, and I put them by themselves for the first time tonight, and they're looking for the rest of their herd."

"Who was that man?" the remaining girl asked.

"No idea," the woman said blithely. "Banged on my window just now and shouted that the ponies were loose. Just had time to get my shoes." She tied tighter the belt of her coat, which could now be seen to be a red dressing-gown. "And Lucy and Mark, where did you spring from?"

"Way home from a party and heard the hooves. Never much liked this skirt, luckily," said the girl, kicking up her hem to show a long rip in it.

"I heard the hooves too," the boy said shyly. "From my bedroom window. And I'd been up to Merriam's with a bit of bread for them before that."

The girl turned on him and said sharply, "Was Merriam's wire all right then?"

"Loopy," said the boy, and a look passed between them that made Elphick wonder. "Shockingly loopy," the woman agreed. "Merriam always was cack-handed. I shoved some bramble across this evening, but I ought to have known it wouldn't hold those two. Officer, I'm so sorry—I'm Mrs. Brooke of Hole Cottage. And I think these are my ponies coming home."

There was a flurry of hooves, and into the light of the car came a cobby little blue, whose cheerful trot was unaffected by the weight of the middle-aged man, who was being half dragged with both arms clasped around its neck.

"You wicked little brute," said Mrs. Brooke with deep affection, and took it by the forelock, saying to the air, "Leading-rein, please." The girl said, "Never much liked this belt either," and gave it to her to loop around the pony's neck. The man, who had hung himself across the pony's withers, said between gulps for air, "Other one's coming. Young lady's getting him bridled."

"What with?" Elphick asked in surprise.

"She wouldn't have come out without something," the woman said, rebuking stupidity. "Why, it's Mr. Tidy, who lent me the long-handled pruner last year. Lovely tool, much better than mine."

"And welcome this year," said Mr. Tidy, and they

plunged into technicalities about pruning, which Elphick interrupted by saying, "Here's the other pony."

It was a leggy little chestnut, wheeling at a canter to avoid the headlights. The pyjamaed girl was riding him bareback with what looked like a head-collar and one leading-rein, and she kept him skipping and sidling on the crown of the road as she called, "Okay, came at once when I whistled. I'll go up and look at Merriam's wire."

"No need, we can bed them down in my shed," said Mrs. Brooke, turning the blue. The rider let the little chestnut dance up to the other girl, stooped to say something brief, and then kicked him on. She seemed to be smiling.

"Where's she going?" Mrs. Brooke demanded.

"Just to make sure of the wire."

"She's going the wrong way then. Jonty!"

She had not gone the wrong way; she had taken the chestnut back to give him room. They heard the thunder of his hooves as she brought him back at the canter and set him at the hedge. In the darkness it seemed an impossible jump; but he was over with a fine flourish of heels and a cowboy yell from the rider, and they heard his hooves going away over soft ground.

In the silence that followed the girl said, "Golly."

"That was some jump," Dickson said admiringly, dismissing the thought that it must have been into the middle of private property.

"Yes, well," said Mrs. Brooke, "let's get back. Come on, you lot; I'll give you a drink at my place."

Elphick, who had been remembering things, said quietly to the boy, "You wouldn't be Mark Pollard by any chance? I believe an officer called at your house when you were away."

"Yes, about poor Jill," the boy said readily. "I only heard about it when I got back, and my parents aren't here yet. I rang Mr. Hobden, and I'm going to see him when my mother gets back in the morning. Won't be any help, I'm afraid, because I was at home and in my dark-room all evening. Have they found out any more about it? Oh, I suppose you can't tell me; sorry."

Elphick was a little impressed. The boy was nothing so much as beautiful, slight for fifteen, with brown hair curl-ing close to his nape and a girl's fringed eyes, and in the company of the others had effaced himself shyly; but spoken to he was calm and direct. Elphick said curiously, "That young lady was up to something, wasn't she?"

"Not really," said Mark. "We're always worrying about the horses." His eyes were still on the hedge that Jonty and the chestnut had taken. He said abruptly, "When she took that hedge, she looked just like Jill."

Elphick was hoping for a transfer to the C.I.D. and meet-ing Cheal next morning he informed him, "Two of your missing witnesses are home again."

"Tell me something I don't know. Hang on, maybe you have. Two? I know about the Pollard boy."

"Well, his dad. Saw Fred Tidy chasing ponies last night."

"Oh, young Chris. Just caught him between fishing and visiting an uncle. Like everyone else, spent the evening at the disco and mooching. So did the Higgins boy. So did the Hewens boy. So did the Crossly boy."

"Can't be wrong with young Mark," hazarded Elphick. "Too calm."

"Mate," said Cheal, "if you'd knocked off the girl-friend on Thursday, by Sunday night you'd have to be very calm, or you'd be a raving nutter."

CHAPTER 6

Cheal invited his superior to interview the Cantrells. "They wouldn't like to think they only rated a sergeant, sir."

Hobden regarded pretty Mrs. Cantrell in a sun-suit on the patio, with the baby kicking and rolling on a rug beside her, both of them a colour that indicated they had spent much of their time here lately, with someone else running the Hoover indoors, and agreed with Cheal.

"Oh, that poor Jill," said Barbara, clearing glossy magazines so that he could sit down: "what an absolutely horrible thing to happen. Some burglar she disturbed, I suppose it was, and I hope you get him quickly. But it's no good asking me anything about it, because I haven't been there for months. I stopped riding before the baby was born, of course, and now I really haven't time."

"That's my mistake, ma'am," Hobden apologized, and made a play of consulting the riders' book so that he could settle into the deck-chair; he did not think the lady would miss the chance of getting a little information from him. "Mrs. Brooke was kind enough to lend me this, and I found your name and your husband's here."

"The dear old book." Barbara sighed pleasantly. "I really should have rung Val, but somehow I never have a moment. It's not fair to forget her, because she was awfully good to me in those miserable days."

"Miserable days, ma'am?"

"When we owned our mare. That was the therapy my husband thought up for me, after I'd had two miscarriages and got myself into a silly state, convinced I couldn't have a baby." She tickled the child, laughing at her own absurdity. "I used to ride when I was at school, but I was too depressed to take much interest until Brian got Val to find me this chestnut, and I absolutely fell for her. Sheba, that was it: I used to ride every day for a bit, and it really did do me good. Brian used to come with me now and again, on Harvey or Ebony. He's a very good rider, and he wanted me to do some jumping and take Sheba to shows. But then I had to give it up when I was pregnant, and though Brian did go for a time by himself, just to get the exercise, it really wasn't worth keeping a horse for the few hours he could fit in; so we sold her." She laughed, inviting him to admire her husband's devotion. "He didn't trust me: that was really what it was; I was so convinced I was going to have a third miscarriage that I wouldn't even admit I was pregnant, and went riding without telling Val I was coming up to three months. I hated losing Sheba; she'd been my comfort for months, and she was a lovely mare; we got sixteen hundred for her, from some people near Petersfield. I did take the baby down to show Val and Kit Cullen, of course, but otherwise I'm afraid I've been rather neglecting them. You know what it's like with a new baby."

Hobden had stopped his eyebrows rising at the mention of Sheba's selling price. There was not even a livery horse at Stumbletts now that would have brought a third of that price. "A thoroughbred was she?" he enquired, calculating in his head.

"Half, I think." And said to have been sold just around the time of Cantrell's involvement with Maxie Fist: useful.

"You knew the dead girl, ma'am?"

"Well, not terribly well, because I was feeling so awful then that I never went out at the week-ends, when there were a lot of riders there; you know how you hate everyone when they're cheerful and you're not. Mostly I went with Val on weekday mornings, when she had one or two nervous adults, like me, who were starting riding again, or when she was just exercising her own horses. Actually it was ages before I managed to make out which was Jill, because there were always the two of them together and everyone called them Jillandjonty. But I know Val thought a lot of her."

"Maybe a word with your husband? If he went on riding after you—"

"Ask him yourself," Barbara said largely, and called into the air, "Brian!"

"I didn't realize he was at home."

"These pilots have odd hours," she said offhandedly.

A tall man looked through the garden doors and said, "Oh, God, not Amber again?" Brown face, brilliant smile, curly black head like a spaniel's: Hobden summed him up in one glance as having too much charm and confidence ever to have needed to be genuinely clever.

"Oh, your dog's safe," Barbara said. "This is Mr. Hobden from the police: my husband."

"Trouble with a dog, sir?"

"He never used to stray, but now Barbara's always with the baby— Amber!"

A handsome yellow Labrador leapt through an open window and threw itself on him, and Barbara pointedly

moved a chair in front of the baby. Cantrell rubbed the
dog's ears in a relief so open as to preclude suspicion that
he had had anything else on his mind. Hobden produced
the riders' book again and explained once more why he
had called, slyly shifting his ground by adding, "With all
the children involved, you'll understand we're finding it
difficult to get adult testimony."

"Oh, poor little Jill. That was a beastly thing. Barbara,
you did at least ring Val?"

"Oh, I will. I really haven't had a moment."

"Then I'll do it," Cantrell said savagely. "But I don't
think we can help. We haven't ridden for—oh, Barbara's
told you. I went a few times after she packed up, just to
keep my weight down, but lately I've been playing
squash, which does the job better; and even then I hardly
saw the poor girl. I couldn't get there for the regular rides,
and I used to go in and take a horse just when I could,
and put the money through the kitchen window. Well, I
felt we owed Val that, because she was good to Barbara.
But it wasn't very satisfactory, because she only has two
horses big enough for me. But you see how it was: I only
saw Jill on the—oh, not more than five or six occasions
when I went on the regular rides with Barbara. I noticed
her, though; you couldn't help noticing her if you knew
anything about riding."

"She was good?" Hobden encouraged him.

"Several of them were *good*; Val's an extremely good
teacher in her slapdash way. The Cullen boy's good, the
girl's going to be better, I think, when she's older; then
there was Jill's friend, whose name I never got right, and
I noticed two of the older girls, Margaret and—Lucy was
it?" He looked at Barbara for confirmation, and Barbara
laughed.

"You can see that my husband is riding-mad, can't

you? I assure you it's not the girls, Mr. Hobden; they're too young for him."

Cantrell went, surprisingly, very red. "I gave up riding when you did," he said to her, with the same savage note in his voice; and to Hobden, faintly apologetic, "Well, if you once fancy yourself at Hickstead you like to pick out the young entry. All I meant was that Jill had something the others hadn't. Class, you'd call it: different in kind, not degree. You'd have thought, to see her at first, that she was just dead reckless; nothing she wouldn't have a try at; but after a bit you could see that she never pushed a horse beyond its powers, never made it mistrust her. A sort of emotional centaur, she was; thought like a horse. . . . But that's all I knew about her, just seeing her ride. Wish we could help you more."

He stood up, and Hobden took the hint. They had after all helped him to some extent. Cheal's notion that Cantrell had been using Stumbletts for an illegal rendezvous was all nonsense. Poor Bert.

There was that extraordinary price for the mare Sheba, though. Could that be significant of anything?

Hardly. There was nothing for it to be significant of, after all. But Hobden decided to present it to Cheal, as a consolation prize.

CHAPTER 7

Not to make too much of a mouthful of it, Valentine went quietly alone to the inquest while Kit did her work at Stumbletts. The Bartons had kept Jonty at home, and Benjamin and Bridie were sent to help their uncle Dave. The amount of work left was overwhelming, and Kit began to calculate when they could get back to summer normal again. There was the blue-eyed cream, unexercised, his careful schooling slipping away now there was no Jill to keep it up. Kit was tempted to bring him out for ten minutes, and with his saddle on her arm had to drop it and run for a customer pulling in at the farm gate.

It was well past noon when Valentine, unfamiliar in the grey she thought proper for a subdued day, came into the shop and said curtly, "What haven't you done?"

"This lot; and I'm panting for some coffee."

"You do the coffee." Valentine plunged into trimming lettuce and watering geraniums. When Kit came back with the two mugs it was done, the floor swept, the counter clear, the board of prices written afresh, but Valentine's lips were tight with fury.

"Drink up. How did it go?"

"Nothing to it. Adjourned on police request for a fortnight." After a deep swig of coffee Valentine relented enough to add, "I talked to Jill's parents."

"Funeral tomorrow?"

"Friday."

Kit put down her mug in dismay. They had agreed that the riding school must not re-open until after the funeral, and the loss of fees would be disastrous. "In heaven's name, why?"

"Cremation and there's a queue. No flowers and private; family only."

"Not us?"

"No."

"Well," said Kit: "well. We are snubbed."

Valentine exploded, "I was bloody thankful! I couldn't have gone into church with that poisonous stepmother!"

"Oh, dear. What happened?"

"I went to talk to her afterwards. Can't hope to say anything adequate, can you?—but just how sorry we were, and how glad to have had her here, and how I thought she'd been happy with the horses. And—oh, *blast* the bitch—"

"She blamed you."

"She did not. She blamed Jill. Always been an impossible girl—obvious for years that something like this would happen—"

"Well, all right," Kit said calmly, as Valentine grew incoherent: "she was only excusing herself. She must know that she—they—neglected her."

"She was talking as if Jill had spent her time smoking hash and watching blue films before going to bed with knife-men. I'm going to buy a cup," said Valentine wildly. "I've worked it out, I'm going to sell the piano and all my own cups, and buy the dirtiest great cup I can find, and call it Jill's Cup for the most outstanding rider, and make it the chief award at our summer show and invite that poisonous woman to present it."

"If we can't open until after Friday, you'll have to sell more than the piano to pay the winter feed bill."

"I won't sell the blue-eyed cream," Valentine said instantly.

Kit took the mugs back into the kitchen and washed them up with something scratching at the back of her mind. Somewhere in that conversation she had for a brief instant remembered the name Jill had given to the blue-eyed cream; but it had gone again. She wondered, probably irrelevantly, what Jill would have been like if her own mother had not died.

Valentine went home before lunch to do her housework, and found her son Caspar tranquilly eating bread and cheese at the kitchen table.

"Mamma," he said, rising to embrace her dutifully, "you should have sent for me."

"My love," said Valentine, her good humour joyfully returning, "what use could that possibly have been? How did you hear?"

"A very small paragraph in a paper I wouldn't dream of reading. One of my students showed it to me."

Caspar's smooth dark hair was cut short, and his beautiful brown-and-oatmeal clothes were of precisely the degree of casualness correct for visiting a mother in the country on a solemn occasion. Valentine and her son were on the best of terms and disagreed on all important matters, in particular about horses. Caspar, who had been able to stay in the saddle before he could safely stay on his feet, thought them a trivial amusement. Valentine, though she had never said so, was amazed that anyone should find archaeology necessary enough to take it up as a life's work. Those who knew them separately could not believe that they were mother and son; yet, unlike as they were, Caspar had his mother's dark caraway-seed eyes, which very occasionally gave him an uncanny resemblance to her.

He helped her to bread and cheese from the table he had laid with exquisite correctness, and they exchanged news as they ate. Valentine gave him an edited version of Jill's death, suppressing her own financial troubles. He was unmarried, but she disapproved strongly of his tendency to be protective towards her. She suppressed also her views on the identity of the murderer. After thought he said merely, "Mamma, I am sure you have no links with crime."

When they had finished he sent her politely into the garden while he washed up and made the coffee; but presently came out to her, not with coffee but with Hobden, who was regarding him with mild surprise.

"We have introduced ourselves, Mamma. Mr. Hobden wished to return something to you."

Hobden was carrying her address book like a passport.

"Sit down," Valentine invited him, "and I'm sure you'd like some coffee. Caspar is just making it."

"I daresay it's private," Caspar said discreetly, "but I shall be just indoors if you need me."

He went away to get the coffee, and Valentine said with a broad smile, "I didn't summon him to protect me, Mr. Hobden."

"I'm sure he'd do it admirably, ma'am, if it were necessary. But I'm glad you didn't, because I have a favour to ask of you."

"Anything I can," Valentine said sunnily, and turned to take the coffee from her son. It was not, of course, in two mugs, but on a tray with her best china. She poured Hobden a cup, and in return he handed over her address book.

"We've found this a great help. What I'd like you to tell me about is something else altogether. I don't know if it affects this case, but I'd just like to tie it up if I could."

"I wouldn't have thought there was anything else."

"We happened, in the course of our enquiries, to interview Captain and Mrs. Cantrell."

As anyone might have expected, Valentine said at once, "What on earth for?"

"We believed, ma'am, that Captain Cantrell continued to ride with you even after their mare was sold."

"Well, he did, but not that much. He'd been used to coming independently when they had Sheba, and he really is a very good rider, and for a short time it was agreed that he could come in and take a horse when he liked. He works shift hours, of course. It wasn't a very good arrangement, because only Ebony and Harvey really suit him, and anyway I suspect he didn't like telling Barbara he'd been riding when she couldn't. I don't think he's been for months."

"I understand you sold a mare for him."

"Yes, Sheba. Not recently, though. The date's in the book."

"I've seen it, ma'am. Would you mind telling me what price you got for her?"

"Yes, I would. Ask him."

"I have, ma'am. I would like your confirmation."

"No. If I do a job for someone, that's between him and me."

"Then can you give me the name of the buyer?"

To his surprise Valentine threw up her hands and laughed at herself. "Well, that's the trouble, isn't it? The wealthy stockbroker in Petersfield with the two horsy daughters: can't do it." She dug a packet of cigarettes out of her shirt pocket and lit one, still smiling. "Look, I'm not going to tell you the price, but you can hear the rest of it if you like, because from where you're sitting it's all rather silly. From where I'm sitting, it meant a lot to Barbara Cantrell."

"If it's not relevant to our enquiries, ma'am, you can trust us to be discreet."

"Oh, it was long before your enquiries, almost a year ago. Goes back even further, really, to when Brian and Barbara were first married. She had two miscarriages and was in rather a state, and when Brian bought Sheba for her she latched on to her in a rather pathetic way."

"She mentioned that she had got very fond of her."

"Yes, I imagine she would. She was a bit purposeful about it, mind you, striking attitudes slightly, but it was all genuine nevertheless. Then she was pregnant for the third time, and Brian persuaded her that they must sell Sheba. It was sensible enough, because she wasn't up to his weight, but he confessed to me that he also needed the money pretty badly. So badly, in fact, that he wouldn't wait for me to look round for a buyer, but insisted I send her to Parsons' next sale and let him have the cheque that very evening. And the reserve he put on her was pitiably low. Well, it was one piece of bad luck on another. Kit fell up the cellar steps and hurt her knee and couldn't drive, and I couldn't go because it was one of our Riding for the Disabled days; the only person I could find who could both drive and handle a horse was a student Kit had here as a paying guest. He was a sensible boy and very anxious to do his best, and we sent two of the lads with him, Chris and Kit's Benjamin, and they had strict instructions to go the minute they got there and find Kit's brother-in-law Dave and get him to help. Well, it wasn't anyone's fault. Dave had got a buyer for his bullocks and kept the boys waiting, and the student let Sheba go at ten above the reserve two minutes before Dave arrived. It was a perfectly legal sale—cash, but most of the sales there are for cash. The only thing that was wrong with it was that the buyer had mentioned a village near Crawley and told a story about a second horse for a wife who was a local show-jumper, and Dave happened to know that that address didn't exist. They'd been fooled, of course, and Sheba had gone to the meat-tin."

"Eh?" said Hobden, confused by this conclusion.

"Bought for slaughter. It's a legal trade, though probably the slaughtering isn't. It's got to the point now where even the farmers, who aren't sentimental about their beasts, won't sell unless they know the buyer. The smaller operators always come with some kind of cover-story. And there's a certain amount of rustling attached, as every horse-owner knows. . . . Well, that's all there was to it. Dave and the boys wasted a lot of time trying to get a line on the buyer, but it wouldn't have been any good. We had to tell Brian what had happened, and it turned out then that he'd promised Barbara that Sheba would only be sold to someone I knew and recommended."

"He hadn't told you that before?"

"No, he hadn't; but then that's Brian. Even when he's honest he's up to some trick or other, even if it's only to keep his hand in. This was all in a good cause, because Barbara would have gone overboard if she'd known what had happened to her mare, but all unwilling I had to go along with him, though I did tell him first what I thought of him. We invented this family with two teenagers who wanted a jumper they could bring on, and luckily it didn't have to last long, because with the baby in prospect Barbara soon got over her passion for Sheba. I suppose you were talking to the two of them and thought Brian sounded a bit edgy on the subject of Sheba."

"No," said Hobden, "not quite. I was talking to Mrs. Cantrell alone, and she told me that Sheba had fetched sixteen hundred pounds. Do you confirm that, Mrs. Brooke?"

After a pause Valentine said, "No, I don't." She looked contemptuous, as well as a little puzzled.

CHAPTER 8

A message was left at the airport inviting Captain Cantrell to call at the police station; which he did in a very bad temper.

"I'm nothing but a witness, and hardly that anyway," he snapped at Hobden. "Will you please not behave as if I haven't paid my motor tax!"

"I'm sorry about that, sir," Hobden said blandly. "We couldn't get in touch with you personally—"

"I was flying."

"And we thought you'd prefer a message left at your place of business rather than at your home."

"Neither would have been necessary if you'd waited a day."

"That wasn't our view, sir. And it seemed to us that you would much prefer your wife not to hear of our enquiry."

"Oh, Christ, now you're going to turn nasty. I am absolutely ready to admit," said Cantrell with force, "that there are things that I would prefer my wife not to hear about, and curiously enough I am not ashamed of all of them. But I am not going to be blackmailed by threats to tell on me."

"That wasn't at all on my mind," Hobden said mildly. "It was Mrs. Brooke asked us not to let your wife know about this."

"Val?" said Cantrell, checking. "Oh, Val's all right; if it was her that— Oh, now I'm with you. Not that damned silly business about Sheba?"

"The sale of that mare, sir, yes."

"Well, if that's all—" Cantrell sat back in his chair and lit a cigarette, offering Hobden one; his ease appeared wholly genuine. "One can rely on Val, but I suppose she didn't hear the whole story about that, or she'd have beaten me up verbally even worse than she did. I thought you were enquiring into poor little Jill's death, though."

"We think there may be a connection." Cantrell pushed out his lips in an expression of disbelief, but waited for the question. "In fact it was your wife who gave us a piece of information we found surprising. She mentioned that the mare Sheba fetched sixteen hundred pounds."

"And Val told you different."

"Mrs. Brooke chose to regard the price as a matter of confidence between the two of you; but her account of the circumstances of the sale confirmed our doubts about the price."

Cheal added bluntly, "They don't pay that high for horse-meat."

"Must you remind me of what happened to Sheba?" Cantrell snapped. "I've ridden ever since I was a boy, and I like horses; the fact that I sold Sheba doesn't mean that I don't regret it. I only hope she got into the hands of a properly licensed slaughterer, that's all. I blame myself, because I needed the money and insisted on selling fast. That's one of the things I'm not ashamed of hiding from my wife."

"We quite understand that, sir. And sympathize, if I may say so. I suppose you told her you got that rather incredible price just to bolster up your story of a kind owner?"

Cantrell looked at him steadily without answering. Finally he said, "Come on. You know a bit more about that than you're letting out. Been following up my debts?"

"Things get around, sir."

"I bet." Cantrell let out a snort of laughter. "Hell, what a stupid tangle. Okay; it was like this. I've a harpy of a divorced wife who strips me of every penny of maintenance she can get. We'd run up the bills a bit more than usual; alterations to the house with the baby expected, and all the baby's stuff to buy, and Barbara was so damned happy after those two miscarriages that I hadn't the heart to tell her we had to cut down; so I needed money a bit more than usual. As it happened, I'd already decided that Sheba had to go. Barbara couldn't ride when she was pregnant, and livery fees plus the baby were beyond me; and just as I'd got Barbara to see it that way I won twenty-two hundred on the horses."

Unseen by Cantrell, Cheal turned up his eyes. Winning on the horses: the one watertight explanation for an acquisition of money; they could not have expected Cantrell to miss that.

"I didn't particularly want to tell her I'd been playing the horses, because she thought I'd given it up, and there was no need for her to worry about money just then. So I kept quiet about that and let her think that Sheba had made enough to pay off the tradesmen. I had to invent an elaborate story about Sheba's new owner after those children botched the sale, but that was only incidental; and by that time Barbara had stopped being depressed and more or less given up horses. So does that satisfy you?"

"Good story, that," Cheal commented with appreciation after he had shown him out.

"Very sound job. Every word of it true, wouldn't you say, bar the provenance of the money?"

"Oh, sure. That twenty-two hundred came from Maxie Fist."

"I don't know what you're looking so pleased about, Bert," Hobden complained. "We're chasing a girl's murderer, happen to remember?"

"First hint we've had of any sort of motive."

"*Any sort of* is a nice way of putting it. All you've done is establish something that happened last year—which we'd pretty well guessed anyway—that has nothing whatever to do with Stumbletts except that slip-up over the sale of the mare. Incidental, just as Cantrell said. He may have no financial morals, but that doesn't make him a murderer."

"I didn't say it was him. Those he's been working with are murderers over and over again, if we could only nail them. And he may not be a murderer, but he isn't the kind that gives up a racket once he's discovered he can make money at it."

"Well, that's true," Hobden admitted. "Yes, I give you that, Bert: I'd be very surprised indeed if our captain really had given up bringing in a little packet of dutiable goods now and again. But I'd be even more surprised if that had anything to do with that poor girl's murder."

"I'd still like to investigate further," Cheal said stubbornly.

"I think you'll be wasting your time. But there; I could be wrong."

"Do no harm, anyway."

Hobden, in the act of clearing up his notes, stopped and gave him a sharp glance.

"Do no harm? Bert, you ought to know better than that."

"Sir?"

"If Cantrell's trying to muscle in on Maxie's racket, Maxie won't like it. And he'll like it even less if he suspects that Cantrell has been grassing on him. Just you look out, Bert; just you please look out."

At about this time Kit was looking in surprise at Valentine bringing Barnaby in from the common. Barnaby was her own little chestnut, a blood pony, so nervous that no one else was allowed to ride him; she had gone out plodding an hour ago, and now was returning at a canter. Seeing Kit at the kitchen window, she flourished her whip and called something that sounded very like, "Sold the cream!"

Benjamin was cleaning his boots, Bridie painting; both looked up startled. Kit went to the door, and behind her heard Bridie say sweetly to her brother, "Did she say sold Fallada?"

"Some good luck!" Valentine announced with Barnaby's saddle over her arm. "Well, kindness really, and you'll never guess who from. Diana Aubrey's getting engaged (I didn't think they did that any more, did you?). You know those people who bought the old oast as a tax-loss farm—Farncombe, isn't it?—their son."

Benjamin had come out, and said, sniffing, "They were at one of the autumn shows last year. Vicuña rugs and cashmere sweaters, and none of them rode."

"Well, Diana doesn't, to any great extent. But Daddy's going to buy her a horse for a wedding present, and the nice child not only asked for the blue-eyed cream, but persuaded him that he might miss it if he didn't buy at once. I'm going round there this evening."

"She *is* nice," said Kit, impressed in spite of herself.

Benjamin said in a tight voice, "And is the cream to go to those non-riders?"

"We must stop calling him the cream; she's got a name for him. Azul. It seems she met her intended in Spain."

"Eh?" said Kit.

"Spanish for blue."

"He isn't a blue."

"Well, they wouldn't call him Blanco."

"I asked—" Benjamin began on a curiously high note.

"Sorry, Benjamin. No, he's staying here at livery."

Benjamin nodded curtly; but he had gone very white. Bridie observed detachedly, "He'd have to stay here until he was schooled anyway. Diana couldn't ride him now. Come on, Benj."

"She's right," Kit said with regret. "Diana on a horse behaves like royalty in a limousine. The cr—no, what was it?—Azul—he's too good for her. She needs a pretty pottering mare, like Snowgoose. Snowgoose would have suited her perfectly."

"Snowgoose is worth one quarter of Azul's price. You keep your tongue off Diana; she's doing me a good turn."

"She did me one over the shop," Kit acknowledged. "Maybe you can bring her on a bit during the summer. How are the bookings?"

"Not too bad considering. We've lost one or two, but they may reappear later, and we've gained one or two I suspect of being ghouls. The five who were here on the Friday it happened were the earliest to ring."

"Thought they would be," said Kit with satisfaction. "I met Mary Rolands in the bank, and she said Jane and Karen were driving her up the wall, hanging around the house with nothing to do."

"They haven't been worried by Jill's death then?"

"Well—the impression I got was that by now they were both very bored by the subject."

"Bored!" said Valentine, slightly shocked. "Well—I suppose that's healthy."

Thinking of the ghoulish bookings, Kit took the opportunity at breakfast-time next morning to speak firmly to her own children.

"Val is starting rides again and she's short-handed, so help at least with the tacking-up, will you? And listen to this, and I'm not going to say it twice. There is to be no talking about Jill. If any of the children try to start, shut them up. If it's adults, say it was very sad and then change the subject; if they go on asking, say in your coldest tones that they had better speak to me about it."

Bridie went off practising cold tones in shrieks of laughter. Benjamin stayed to ask, "Does that mean we're free of the fuzz?"

"Your guess is as good as mine. I hope the worst's over."

"It was interesting," Benjamin said judicially, "but it got to be a bore. Nothing ever came of it, I mean. Look, we don't have to do more than help tack up, do we?"

CHAPTER 9

The funeral over, Jonty returned to her old bedroom in Hole Cottage.

"She do so insist," Mrs. Barton told Valentine on the telephone. "We thought it'd be sad-like for her, specially a-nights when she'd be alone, but that's young Jonty, as you know as well as any, Mrs. Brooke. Smile and smile and not one word, but what she wants to do she do do."

Had Jonty imagined what it would be like in the evenings without Jill? Valentine began to plan a different kind of evening (which was not easy in Hollow Cross), and then stopped. Was Jonty coming back because she wanted the evenings to stay the same? She realized in dismay that she simply did not know.

She had to take refuge in a fortunate accident.

"Lucy's birthday," said Jonty at breakfast, wrapping up an assortment of make-up. "No party, though; brother's got chicken-pox."

"Have you had it?" Valentine asked. "Have her down here, then, and I'll clear out to Kit's and let you have a cook-up to yourselves."

"Oh, ta; lovely," said Jonty with her faint smile; and

five minutes later said precisely the same thing when offered honey. When the evening came, Valentine filled her refrigerator with sausages, frozen chips, and ice cream, and, reluctant to sully a fine evening with petrol, walked down Hole Lane to Stumbletts, thinking about the girl. That round childish face, with the lips drifting so naturally into the faint smile—quite unchanged, quite unchanged!

Well, what change had she expected?

Again, she simply did not know. "I think I've been flattering myself," she concluded glumly. "Got on with them all right—chiefly because I left them alone—so I conceived the mad idea that I understood them. Oh for God's sake, woman—did you ever understand your own closely studied son?"

She shared Kit's supper and washing-up, and, leaving her with her ironing and a play on the radio, went into the stable yard and decided to clean tack. Dandy, who had followed her expecting to be put on guard, saw that the stable gate was still open, and went back to Kit and the cool flags of the kitchen floor. Dragging out a hay-bale so that she could work in the yard, Valentine wondered how she was going to survive the rest of the holidays short-handed. Benjamin and Bridie could not be relied on for long, and in any case were too young to take leading-reins, which was the great need when there were beginners riding. The Rolands lot, the five who had been here when Jill's body was found, had worked well today, each of them walking with a beginner, but they could not be expected to come every day. Lucy had come; Margaret had been trapped by a family occasion. Not one of the boys had come; with the exception of Mark the other night, she had not seen one of them around since Jill's death.

And some time or other she must give some thought to

the longer-term problem of running the school without Jill. But that was a problem she had been prepared for from the beginning. If there was one thing you learnt in teaching, it was that everyone was temporary. Jill would have got older and gone; Jonty would get older and go. Others would appear in their places.

The reason why she did not want to think very hard now about replacing Jill was sad and simple. Whatever the new arrangement, her optimistic nature would compel her to find advantage in it; and she knew that nearly all the advantages she could find would be genuine. No replacement she could imagine would ride with such inspiration as Jill; but then a child's riding school like hers did not need inspired riding. It needed someone easy, patient, friendly; and Jill had been none of those.

So just for the short time she would go on as they were. If there were too many leading-reins, she would school rather than hack; she would work a little longer herself.

And somehow she would buy that cup, and institute Jill's Award at her next summer's show; and—her spirits, as always, were rising after a fall—when the inevitable happened and kind little Diana Aubrey realized that the blue-eyed cream was too much for her, she would somehow buy him back.

She spent a little time thinking gratefully of Diana, and wondering why she had to waste herself on the plump-jowled Farncombe son. There had been a time, around ten years ago, when she had watched sentimentally her teen-aged Caspar riding ahead of her with Diana; but that pretty picture had only lasted until the moment she saw Caspar's grimly composed face (Caspar's manners had been perfected by the time he was four).

Azul: could she persuade Diana to change the name before it stuck? If someone would only tell her what had been Jill's name for the cream, Diana might agree to it out of sentiment. Benjamin and Bridie ought to know it; so must Jonty; but she was taking pains not to mention Jill to them unless she must. And she had besides a faintly guilty conviction that she had once known it herself, and let it slip out of her mind; had once heard Jill using it, schooling the horse in the yard in the mornings. A nice memory, that, because she was marvellously good with the nervous beast. She used her voice a lot: talked to him all the time.

What *was* that name?

Into Valentine's mind, as she sat on her hay-bale under the darkening sky and rubbed dust from bridles, there came a remarkably unpleasant picture. An arch that led into a stable yard; a procession of riders going below; and nailed above the arch the severed head of a horse.

She came to herself with a jump to find that it was too dark to go on working. The lamp over the tack-room door was burning, and so was one low down in the kitchen window, which meant that Kit had finished her ironing and moved to the table. She had switched off the radio, and everything was very silent; not even the sound of traffic on the coast road.

Or only one car, a powerful one, coming from the north very fast.

Methodically collecting her cleaning brushes and sponges into their basket, she waited for it to pass.

With a startling burst of noise in the quiet night, it wheeled into the stable yard. She saw the driver struggling to straighten; then he pulled on the parking brake, switched off his engine, and let his head fall on to the wheel.

The car was a blue Porsche, a new model, and the head, of course, was Brian Cantrell's.

Valentine said briskly, "Come on then, Brian, no histrionics. Nothing wrong with you if you can drive at that speed."

Cantrell lifted his head blindly and showed her the wreck of his right arm. The thin sweater was in bloodstained strips; from shoulder to elbow were four parallel slashes.

"Original sort of weapon," he said with fair calm. "Wondered why he was wearing only one glove. Razor blades right across it, stood up as he opened his hand."

Her hands were too dirty to touch the arm, but she brushed aside the torn sleeve with the back of her wrist.

"Not too bad," he said. "He was a bit previous, and these windows go up fast. I hadn't switched off, either. I was in a hurry, and thought they'd only flagged me down to ask the way. There are five of them, Val, in a Range Rover. They're after me. I need help."

Valentine looked him over thoughtfully. The head-on-wheel gesture had been histrionics; he was no more than a little cut and shocked. "What have you been up to?" she asked.

"Nothing; bit of fiddling. Not drugs, Val, I swear I wouldn't touch drugs myself. But they thought I was trying to—that business of Jill's, the police have been seeing me—they thought I was grassing on them. They're a nasty lot, Val, and not far behind me."

Valentine stepped back. "Then you had better go away quickly, Brian."

Kit appeared silently at her shoulder, Dandy stalking at her side. She had heard everything, for she was rigid with fury. She said, "Very quickly, Brian."

"I can't," said Cantrell. "I'm almost out of petrol."

Valentine leant across him to look at the dashboard dials. "Yes, he is," she said to Kit.

Totally expressionless, Kit said, "Get it into his head

that I'm not helping him to anything at all. I'm ringing
the police."

Cantrell tried to grasp at her. "Kit—please—"

Kit flicked him off. "My children are in the house. Get
him out of here, Val." She stalked into the house, Dandy
at her heel, and shut the door hard after her.

"Val!" said Cantrell, seizing her. He winced a little,
she noted, but could use his right arm.

"All right," she said, "I get it. The police are no more
welcome than the lot in the Range Rover. It's your choice.
I've a couple of gallons in a can. I'll get it."

"I don't want petrol." Cantrell slid out of the Porsche.
"This thing wouldn't notice two gallons, and they know
I'm on this road. I want a horse, Val."

She stared at him. A horse against a car? Against a
Range Rover that could cover rough ground? But as she
thought of where they were she began to see why he had
come to her. Behind Stumbletts was the strip of common
and farming land and old road, three miles wide, hope-
lessly confusing to those who did not know it, simplicity to those who did. Brian knew it, having ridden in it;
but her horses knew it inch from inch. He could vanish
from sight—

"Come on," he said. "Ebony: where is he?"

"A nice idea, but no. I'm not getting mixed up with
you, Brian. Too dangerous."

He grinned at her; he was very pleased with himself.
"Much more dangerous not to, darling. They're much
closer than the police, and they're looking for this car.
Going to risk having them in here?" He tipped his right
elbow to show her the razor-cuts.

"No," Valentine said composedly, "I suppose I can't.
But before you get any horse of mine that car's got to be
out of my yard."

"I haven't time!" Clever as he thought himself, he was more frightened than he wanted to show.

"Then you haven't Ebony. And you can't get him without me. Out! First field-gate to the south. Pull right off the road, bog yourself if you must, they'll see it anyway. Turn back to your left and follow the hedges; fifty yards along the road and then uphill. Look for me there. *Move it.*"

He stared at her for a wild instant, and then obeyed.

In the suddenly empty yard, with the snarl of the car sinking into the silence, Valentine said to herself, "Now gently." There were things that must not be forgotten. There was a mucking-out bucket in the yard. She emptied it over the tyre-tracks in the dust of the entry, shut and locked the gate, and, taking two bridles from the tack-room, shut and locked the tack-room and turned off the light. It was a clear fine night, and she would be able to see well soon, though now she had to grope for the catch of the home-field gate. She whistled her familiar chirruping call, and soft snorts and wet noses came obligingly out of the darkness to her. There was Ebony's ghostly white blaze; she grasped at his forelock and looked round for a mount for herself. It would have to be her precious Barnaby, the only one fast enough for what she meant to do. If he had one of his fits of terror she would have to sit it out and pray, and it would do no harm to her plan.

Besides, Barnaby would stand to be bitted by her, and struggling with Ebony's bridle in the dark she was having to keep one knee on the gate to stop the rest of them crowding out. She butted them back, got Ebony and Barnaby through and the gate closed, and used a bar of it to help her vault on Barnaby. Leading Ebony, she trotted gently on the path to the common.

Kit had turned out every light in Stumbletts. Somewhere in the still summer air she could hear the insect trill of a powerful engine approaching.

She lost it in a moment, as she turned into the silver birches and gorse coverts of the common. Her private gap through the hedge and down and up a ditch under low oaks was difficult enough to negotiate without Ebony objecting at the stretch of her arm; she hauled him after her with her eyes and hair full of twigs, and emerged on to five acres of pasture. She could not hear engines, but there was no sense in crossing the field. She turned uphill in the shadow of an untrimmed wealden hedge, thorn and holly, head-high to her, mounted, with great oaks here and there; along the top; and then another tricky jog and slither down and up from an overgrown ditch with six inches of mud to be hopped over at the bottom. No need to remind Barnaby or Ebony of that; her horses knew what they were doing. Somewhere along this hedge dipping to the road Brian should be making his way uphill. She walked Barnaby down in shadow until a white smudge rose from it and became Brian's face.

"Val—Val—good!" he said, and as she hauled Ebony up and held out the reins he caught her hand and gave it a warm pressure. Saintly simplicity, she supposed drily, that he should now treat her as a valued ally. Just as well, though, that he should be confident, for she was trusting him with one of her horses. He had nothing to help him mount, and vaulting aboard made him gasp a little and fold over the arm held tightly to his side, but he settled himself well and gathered Ebony, putting out a hand to warn her. "Gently; they're here."

The curve of the hedge had hidden the lights below. For the first time Valentine felt the prickle of immediate personal fear. It helped her. She had ridden and hunted too much not to be able to deal with that, and it blanketed her pressing sense of Stumbletts lying open and unprotected but for Kit and Dandy.

"My poor car," Brian murmured with a laugh.

The Range Rover had been pulled in with its head-lights on the Porsche. One man was still at the wheel, two outside, conferring or casting about, and the other two methodically wrecking the Porsche. She let out a breath as the windows starred and then blackened.

"Frighteners," said Brian cheerfully.

She knew that much; she was seeing the comfortable kitchen at Stumbletts.

"How did you fool them past the farm?"

"Horse-shit," Valentine said with sudden crispness. The word seemed to her well placed, and she touched Barnaby to turn him. "Listen now. Up the side of this hedge, right? On Ebony you're invisible if you keep in shadow, and walk him until you're over the top and you won't be heard even if they've stopped their engine. At the top, bear right forty yards and you'll find a gap. It's miry, but let Ebony take it, he knows it well. Beyond there the broadest ride takes you half a mile to the old railway track. From there on you're on your own, and I've no doubt you'll manage, but one warning: that's my horse you're riding."

She saw the gleam under his shadowed brows as he switched his gaze from the Range Rover to her. "I might need you again, Val? Point taken. I'll find a phone and get a cab to pick me up. I'll try to tether Eb where he can graze and ring you to let you know where. Hey, they're on the move."

The Range Rover had backed away from the Porsche and swung in a wide curve to face up the field, and the four men were climbing in. "They've seen the track," said Valentine, alert and gathering Barnaby. "Okay, not up the field. Off you go."

"What about you?"

Genuinely concerned for her, of course; but of course well behind his care for himself. No use to tell him that she needed him out of the way to make sure the frighteners did not approach Stumbletts. She doubled her reins and swung them at Ebony's rump, saying, "Walk on, Eb." The black horse melted into the darkness.

"Now, my Barny!" said Valentine, and trotted him forward into the field. The track the Range Rover was following was enough to fool townees, being merely the way Dave Cullen had taken his tractor up with feed for his bullocks. When they saw it ending in a turning-circle they would come back; and remember the farm along the road.

She sprang Barnaby to an easy canter, crossing the field openly, well above the Range Rover. Would they hear the hooves above the engine-noise? Yes, all right; they had come to a stop at the turning-circle, and one man was out. Better if she were seen, but how near did she dare get? What was the range of a shotgun? She had no idea. Barnaby was enjoying himself wildly, and she let him out, thundering at full speed past the Range Rover and towards the far fence. No shotguns, thank heaven, but it was in gear and roaring after her with unnerving quickness. "That's my Barnaby! But gently—*now!*"—sitting down hard as they came down on the spot she had had in mind all along, a gap in the hedge that in the dark must look like an open gate. She did not dare give away the trap by pulling Barnaby in hard, but he had decided that he was not going to be stopped; he shortened his stride precipitously, took off at the last possible moment to clear the six feet of springs and brambles and unavailing railway sleepers, and rocketed into the darkness of the next field. Valentine brought him up slowly, rejoicing.

Last time Dave had attempted that gap he had bogged himself for three hours.

She turned Barnaby uphill, which finally persuaded him back to a walk, and breathed him in the shadow of the top hedge, trying to make out what went on below. The driver was good; he knew when wheel-spinning became mere bad temper. From the maze of shadows and low-lit movement she worked out that he had got the other men out to heave, and were laboriously freeing the car. No objection to that, since they had seen, as they thought, Brian riding away south; they would get back on the road and follow him south, away from Stumbletts. And by now surely the police should be arriving? There was no telling whether they would come along the south road, but Valentine's place now, she decided, was between the frighteners and Stumbletts.

She trotted Barnaby back along the top hedge, keeping one eye on the activity below and glowing inwardly at Barnaby's performance, humming softly her only song, which was, "Oh Barnaby, my Barnaby," to the tune of *O Tannenbaum*. There went the Range Rover, free at last, but using its spotlight and backing and filling very cautiously indeed to turn.

What now? Another soft spot?

It had stopped. The engine was off. A figure came into the headlights, one of the men who had been out piloting; it had one hand up, swinging on its heel to look all round.

Look, when he had been in the beam of the headlights?

No; he was listening. He was beckoning. He was springing back into the Range Rover, pointing urgently. In the seconds before its engine snarled up to full revs, Valentine heard what he had heard: the drum of galloping hooves.

Well, Brian had fooled her.

She turned Barnaby to watch, sitting slack in her dis-

gust at him and at herself. Why had she not guessed that
he would always think himself a little cleverer than everyone else? Not enough for him to have his skin saved; he
must try to throw even her off his trail. She supposed that
he was on the run from the police as well, the fool; he had
doubled back to make his escape in a different direction.

And, damn him, on her horse.

And he was not going to do it. Barnaby went up in the
air as she kicked him instinctively forward and then
reined in. Brian had feinted towards the road, drawing
the Range Rover roaring after him, and now was bearing
hard left and making for the lowest part of the hedge into
the next field. A superficial trick leaving the frighteners
stranded by a hedge they could not cross. But nor could
he. Valentine knew that hedge in its every yard; it was
neither laid nor trimmed, the ditch below was rank and
full, six weeks' rain had brimmed until the bog spread out
on all sides; and Brian was trying to take it in the
dark. She remembered, later, that she had cried loudly,
"Ebony!"

But Ebony cleared it, disdainfully, with feet to spare. It
was easy for him; he had shed his rider; who had, after
all, suffered a razor attack not long before and was riding bareback. Most likely, Valentine thought, again later
when she had time to think at all, he had lost control well
before take-off. In the beam of the bearing-down headlights he seemed to lose balance in the turn, to roll off and
lie stunned. She hoped he was stunned; for as he lay there
the Range Rover went four-wheel deliberately over him.

She had a faint idea that the frighteners lingered for
some time around the body, looking it over without
touching it, going to stare at the hedge, lighting cigarettes
and holding brief conversations. She was not sure; she
was dismounted, with her arm round Barnaby's neck. It

was only when she heard the engine again that she re-
joined the world.

She surprised herself a little by her steady hands. She
remounted and trotted gently down the field, patiently
holding Barnaby in check until the driver had found the
gate to the road and decided which way he was going. He
chose to go north, towards Stumbletts. It did not worry
her. She would have them whichever way they went. She
let Barnaby show his speed again parallel with the road.
At the gate before Stumbletts, Dave Cullen had been
dumping hard core to firm the mire. She was off before
Barnaby had come to a halt, and had her hands on a half
breeze-block that fitted her arm nicely. She could not
remount carrying it, but she jammed it into the hedge,
vaulted up, leant over and rolled it into the crook of her
left arm. Leaning a little to compensate for the weight,
she set Barnaby cantering along the road hedge. She
could hear the engine somewhere behind her, but she
knew the spot she wanted, and as she neared it pulled
Barnaby away from the hedge and kicked him on. He
hardly needed it; he was almost full out. She took him in
a wide turn uphill and bore straight down on the hedge,
setting him hard at it while her right hand went under
the breeze-block on her left arm.

Barnaby was enjoying himself. He picked his heels up
over the hedge and landed perfectly in the road beyond,
and then realized disastrously that a glaring vehicle was
coming up on his near side. As his fore-legs went up, Valentine got her hand round the breeze-block and shot it, as
hard as she could, straight across her at the glaring headlights. She heard the crash and shatter as it hit, but could
not see past the lights; and anyway had no leisure for
looking, because she was lying half-off Barnaby's neck,
one hand tight in the mane, while he bolted wildly down
the road past Stumbletts.

The practical Kit had telephoned the police, locked the
shutters, put the shotgun and all her torches on the
kitchen table, got out the first-aid box and the brandy,
and filled the coffee-pot. It did not surprise her that Valentine had not followed her into the house, but the long
silence after that made her uneasy. She rang the police
again.

"Nearest car's about a mile from you, Mrs. Cullen."

They were not using the siren, and she wished they
would, to break the silence. She checked that both her
children were asleep and their doors closed. Then she
heard a horse going past the house at a speed that
brought her to her feet. It was gone before she could get
to a gap in the shutters. "If it was Val on him," she
thought forlornly in the silence, "I suppose she can't have
come to much harm?"

And there at last was the police siren, and she could
open her door.

They were not helpful when she demanded what had
happened, and presently she realized that this was because they did not know. Hobden seemed to be there,
and his rosy-faced sergeant, and she grew bewildered;
and also, with the relief from the tension, angry. This had
surely nothing to do with Jill's death? Or was every type
of crime Hobden's pigeon? And it was her house, wasn't
it, her land—her danger? What right had they to tell her
nothing? And then Valentine trudged down the road
leading Barnaby, and after one look at her face Kit forgot
her anger and went quickly to get her coffee that was half
brandy.

Valentine was very quiet and extremely polite. She said
to Kit, "I led Barny for the last half-mile, but he's been
down. Would you be very kind and look him over for
me?" She looked a little battered herself, and Kit hurried
over to Barnaby and ran back to the kitchen and her first-

aid box. Valentine was taking long draughts of the doc-
tored coffee and paying no attention to an exasperated
Hobden or half a dozen others bustling in and out. "Too
kind," she murmured distantly as Kit pushed her way in
and started bathing an arm grazed from wrist to shoulder.

Ignoring the police, she said, "I suppose you came off?"

"No," said Valentine unoffended. "I had to bush Barny
to get him off the road, and his feet went from under him
in a boggy patch. Is he all right?"

"Perfectly."

"Good. And where please is my black horse?" She fixed
Hobden with a glance that was slightly mad in its glassy
calm.

"Ebony?" said Kit; and, since no one else seemed to
know anything, guessed wildly, "You gave Ebony to
Brian?"

"He's got away?" Hobden exclaimed.

Valentine looked away from him. "You haven't found
him. First field-gate on the left and along the hedge. But I
won't show you where."

Hobden started directing his men out. "Ma'am," he
said with surprising gentleness to her, "what happened to
him?"

"Oh, I should say he's dead," Valentine said offhandedly. In precisely the same tone she added, "I suppose
I've killed someone too?"

"No, ma'am. You did a nicely judged job. Windscreen
crazed, vehicle in the ditch, a few broken bones, and five
men in police custody. I'd be light with the brandy, Mrs.
Cullen, and get her to bed as soon as you've strapped up
those scratches. I'll see her in the morning."

Valentine said loudly, "And where is my black horse?"

It was daylight before Hobden came back, and then he
was brief and preoccupied. "I'll need a witness statement

from Mrs. Brooke. I take it she's here?—I'll be in touch later today, when she's had her sleep out. Not a lot of doubt what happened, and it looks as if she's to be congratulated."

"I don't think she sees it like that."

"Perhaps you'd like to tell her that we know these villains, and Cantrell wasn't the only one. We've no news of the black horse, I'm afraid, but I'd guess he bolted southerly. I'll have him looked out for, but you can probably do as well for yourself by ringing your neighbours in that direction."

"I'll do that. And, Mr. Hobden?"

"I'm very pressed, ma'am."

"Don't worry, so am I," Kit said tartly. "Just answer me one question, please. This can't be connected with Jill?"

"We have been investigating the possibility. Innocently on her part."

CHAPTER 10

It had always been one of the blessings of Kit's life that her children were sound sleepers. By the time they were down for breakfast, the house was clear of all signs of the night's alarms; but there was still a police presence around the wreck of the Porsche up the road.

"There's been a car crash outside. You're not to go out on the road today."

To forbid Benjamin to do something was to infect him with the passionate conviction that this was the one thing he must on no account fail to do. "How are we to exercise if we can't go on the road?"

"Go," Kit advised him crisply, "in the opposite direction. Nothing to do with me, my son. The police are there."

"And will tell you to go away," Bridie confirmed, scraping the honey-jar.

Kit turned to stare at her.

"I tried," Bridie said sweetly.

This silenced Benjamin; but half an hour later he skidded in to the dairy, demanding, "Where's Ebony? What have you done with Ebony?"

"Oh-I-give-*up*!" stormed Kit, slamming down a petunia. Mother and son glared at one another. Simultaneously they said, "Well, I didn't mean—" and, "Oh well, I suppose—"

"No, you," said Benjamin, who knew an advantage when it was his.

Kit, who knew an ally when she needed one, said, "Look, you can be intelligent when you try. I don't mind your knowing, but I won't have you joining in and I don't want Bridie frightened. Granted?"

"I'll look after Bridie. Granted."

"Then last night there was a bit of a crisis."

"You got the shotgun down." Grudgingly, Benjamin acknowledged, "Bridie saw that. It was dusted."

"Damn. I did get it down, but that was sensationalism. I'd already rung the police, and anyway Val coped."

"What *with*?"

"Well—crime. The organized stuff: for money. I don't know quite what kind, but it was Brian Cantrell. He was killed."

Benjamin's eyes opened enormously. "Was he a goody or a baddy?"

"There were degrees, I think. A baddy, but not as baddy as the organized lot."

"Had he been a bit of a fool?"

"Splendid; continue to be as intelligent as that, my son. He struck you like that? Yes, he had been more than a bit of a fool, and it caught up with him."

"That reads." Benjamin thought it over, his eyes gleaming with interest. "And it killed him, and you and Val coped? Good for the old ladies!" He creased his eyes at her in his highest expression of approval. "All to do with Jill?"

"The police seem to think so."

"Too much of a coincidence if it wasn't. She got in the

way somehow. Oh, terrific. Wish I'd seen it all." He was at his sunniest; then clouded. "But how does Ebony come into it? What's happened to him?"

"Oh, shush; nothing. Brian was riding him, and he went loose afterwards. It was way towards your uncle Dave's place, and I've rung him and the police are looking out. He'll be picked up soon."

"Yes," said Benjamin. He stuck his hands casually into his pockets. "Well, ta for telling me, mum." He strolled to the door and then took off from his toes.

By the time Hobden telephoned Valentine had woken and was eating scrambled eggs. Kit asked her, "Sure you can take him? Then in about half an hour, Mr. Hobden?"

Valentine, if not cheerful, was decisive again. "Get it over and done with, shall we?"

"You think this will do it?"

"Don't you, love?"

"Well, he wants a witness statement from you—me too, I suppose; which means there'll be court cases against those men—"

"I didn't mean that."

"I've got muddled," Kit complained. "What had Brian done? I know he was a slippery customer, but—"

"He'd been a fool," said Valentine, showing a remarkable resemblance of mental process to Benjamin's. "He let it out to me in the yard. He'd been smuggling. He swore it wasn't drugs, which probably means that it was, once; and he'd got in with more than he'd bargained for. I suppose he thought it was possible to make a quick dip into organized crime and forget about it as soon as he'd got his quick quid."

"Oh. And what has that to do with Jill?"

Valentine pushed away her plate and took an apple

from the bowl. "Jill happened to be around when she wasn't wanted."

"Why wasn't she wanted?"

"Don't be stupid."

"Jill was in a stable a few yards from an occupied house, in a neighbourhood where everyone knows everyone else's business—"

"Yes, well, we know all that bit."

"And behind a gate where there was a dog who wouldn't have let any stranger in without barking the place down. Val, you don't believe this any more than I do."

"No," said Valentine, "of course I don't. But everyone else will."

"You still think one of the stable-lads killed her."

"Yes."

"And you're going to leave everyone else thinking—"

"Yes."

"Val, you mustn't."

"You think so?" said Valentine, like a crackle of static on the radio. "I don't. I used to think I didn't, and now I know I don't. And I'm not arguing about it."

"*Now?*"

Valentine shut her mouth, like one who has said enough. Kit was mercilessly silent. Finally Valentine said, "Having felt momentarily murderous myself. And having acted upon it."

Kit stared, understood, and exploded. "I have never heard such nonsense! You put a load of criminals into a ditch, which was less than they deserved. That wasn't murderousness, it was justice."

"Like to bet," Valentine offered, "that every murderer hasn't thought he was doing justice?"

"You didn't kill anyone."

"Sheer incapability. I meant to."

There was a long silence. Kit said at last, "But it *has* to be the same killers both times! Benjamin saw it. Too much of a coincidence if it wasn't, he said. A month ago, would you have believed it if you were told we had *one* killer here?"

"No."

"And now you say we have two. Is it a good season or something?"

But Valentine shook her head, even smiling a little.

"No, love. You've missed a point. Brian's death following Jill's wasn't coincidence. It was consequence."

"Consequence of her death? How?"

"We were connected with his fiddlings because we sold Sheba for him and he told lies about it. I think the police must have had some suspicions of him earlier, because they investigated those lies rather thoroughly. They visited his house; they called him to the station; they probably made some pointed enquiries about his financial affairs. So the drug-peddlers thought he was grassing on them, and killed him for it."

When Hobden arrived, he confirmed that he needed a statement from Kit as well.

Kit cursed; she was already behind with her work.

"Then Benjamin will have to mind the shop," and she went to find him.

He was not to be seen; but humming in the big stable was Jonty, who had taken the ten-thirty ride in the school. "Benjamin?" she said placidly. "Gone out somewhere. With Bridie, I think. Anyway Mouse and Cupid are gone."

"Blast the boy. Can you mind the store, Jonty?"

Kit had hardly finished with Hobden and seen him off when a very stiff Mary Rolands was on the telephone.

"Mrs. Cullen, have you got my girls?"

"Jane and Karen?—no. They weren't booked in, were they?"

"No, they weren't. But they've rushed off on their bikes without a word to me, and I know they were talking to your Benjamin not long before."

Kit knew better than to defend Benjamin without full knowledge of all his movements. "They would hardly be coming here, Mrs. Rolands, on their bikes. It's all of eight miles."

"And they're not allowed on the coast road because of the traffic. Well," said Mary, weakening, "I'm sorry to have troubled you."

But soon others were troubling Kit. It was Tina, the youngest of the five, who gave the game away. In summoning her to his private purposes, Benjamin had forgotten that she was young enough to be missed very quickly. Her small bicycle was seen propped against a field-gate, and she was overtaken industriously quartering a nearby coppice and calling for Ebony. She protested so violently that she had to be carried home kicking, which so impressed her mother that she too got on the phone to Stumbletts.

"Mrs. Cullen, I hope I'm not being silly—"

"I doubt it," said Kit grimly.

"—but you've got a horse called Ebony, haven't you? Tina seems to be worried out of her mind that he has been stolen and will end up, as she puts it, in the meattin. She says that everyone is out looking for him."

"She seems to be right," said Kit, and started telephoning herself.

Benjamin had turned out every rider he could get in touch with, and, what was startling, even those who were on bad terms with him (roughly two-thirds of them) had gone at once.

"Are all these children out of their tiny minds?" Kit stormed to Jonty.

Valentine had been sent home to do her housework and cook supper. Jonty said in her quiet way, "They're all bothered about the meat-tin men."

"Did Benjamin come to you?" Kit accused her.

Jonty said scrupulously, "No. But I was schooling with the ride. I'll take Gingerbread and look for them."

By the mercy of heaven (as Kit said bitterly later) no child was reported missing to the police, though there were some near shaves, and it was Jonty who found Ebony, though one of the children had got there first. Reckoning that Benjamin would have gone south towards Dave Cullen's land and then borne off east to the common land, where a horse could stray grazing unseen for hours, she took a short cut by way of the old road as far as Hugletts Bridge, where by dismounting and leading her horse down the steep descent she reached the farm road below and went at a brisk canter into the farther reaches of the common, where they seldom rode. Here her persevering calls were soon rewarded by a shout, and she found the stolid straw-haired Amanda trudging along leading Ebony.

"And what did Madam have to say?" Kit demanded.

"She said, 'I've found him and I've got blisters.' She wanted to ride him, but couldn't find anywhere to mount."

"Thank heaven for that, then. She couldn't manage Eb. And how did she manage to get so far from home?"

"Told her mum she'd been invited to the Pagetts' and was driven nearly to the spot."

"And what did you do with her?"

Jonty regarded her calmly, her lips lifting into her faint ironic smile. "Put her up on Ebony and dropped her round the corner from her home. She said it would be all right."

Amanda must have concealed her blisters; no complaint came from her mother. When Valentine heard about the search, she laughed joyfully.

"Oh, Kit, I know it must have worried you, but you must admit they're resourceful."

"Benjamin was sent smartly to bed without supper, and pay and privileges docked for a week. You're soft on them, Val."

"Maybe. All the same—funny they're so concerned, isn't it?"

CHAPTER 11

The summer holiday went on. Familiar faces disappeared for a week, postcards arrived, the faces returned browner. It was a good summer, wet enough to keep the grass growing, sunny enough to keep the riders coming. Slowly Valentine's bookings picked up, and somehow they kept the school running short-handed. Margaret and Lucy faithfully arrived every morning and stayed all day, and after a week or so three of the young ones, Tracey, Jane, and Karen, unearthed a cousin who had started work in the town and was willing to give them transport. They managed the rides by cutting down on the stable-work, and Valentine did that by starting at seven in the morning and finishing when it was too dark to see. Kit began to worry about her gaunt look.

Neither Paul, Kevin, Colin, Chris, nor Mark appeared. Lucy said scornfully one day, "Can't expect the boys to turn to and help, can you?"

"Well, you can't," said the sensible Margaret. "Kevin and Colin are working, Paul lives twelve miles away, and Chris and Mark are on holiday."

"Kevin and Colin are mostly lounging around that

awful yard of theirs; and Mr. Tidy's not on holiday, I saw him yesterday."

"There's an uncle Chris goes fishing with. Anyway," said Margaret, abandoning justice, "they're not much good when they are here, though it would be handy to have someone else to lead now and again."

Three days later Lucy turned up in the morning with Mark in tow.

"They said you were on holiday," Valentine remarked.

"That's my parents," Mark said shyly. "I've been here all the time. I bought a new lens for my camera so I couldn't afford a ride, but Lucy says you could do with some help."

"Be our guest," said Valentine, and Mark continued to come each day. The winter-feed account grew: too slowly, but it grew.

At the resumed inquest on Jill's death, the police requested a further adjournment.

Kit had a curious encounter a couple of days after this. Doing her weekly late-night shopping at the supermarket in the town, she stopped to talk to the deceptively gentle-looking organizer of Riding for the Disabled, and found that it was Detective Chief Inspector Hobden who was patiently holding carrier-bags to unload her trolley into.

"I believe you know my husband?"

"Is Mr. Hobden your husband? I mean," said Kit foolishly, "*this* Mr. Hobden? I simply didn't connect you."

"It's always better," said Mrs. Hobden briskly. "If they did connect us, half my friends would never speak to me again, and the other half would want to speak to me far too much."

But Hobden left her to carry two bags and relieved Kit of hers; a movement marked enough for Kit to speak to him directly as he waited for her to open her car.

"Mr. Hobden: what is happening about Brian Cantrell's death?"

Hobden rubbed his hand where the carrier had cut it, and said mildly, "You must have realized, Mrs. Cullen, that you were lucky over that. He died just off your land."

"Yes, I did. It helped with the local papers; they kept off. But all we know is the adjournment of Jill's inquest."

"Well, rolling up the Maxie Fist gang is a long business. I think I told you at the time: we've a lot against them, and this looks like the chance to make a great deal of it stick. We're not at all sure, unfortunately, that we can get them on either murder charge."

"But Val *saw* them kill Brian."

"And Mrs. Brooke wouldn't be a witness easy to move. It's the question of intent that worries us. Since they didn't back up and make a separate run at him, we don't think we can prove intent to kill; they could argue that he fell under their wheels. And of course with the girl it's even worse. But there will be other charges, and serious ones; they won't get away with it. It will be some time before it comes to court."

"I suppose we should be thankful for that," said Kit, pondering; so that she was unprepared when he launched his next question.

"That boy of yours, Mrs. Cullen: would you recognize his handwriting if you saw it?"

Kit stiffened; *now* what had Benjamin been doing? "I don't know. I might say if it wasn't his; but there's this fashion for italic, and his changes all the time."

"Ah; no expert will tackle a child. I'm sorry, Mrs. Cullen—that was just a remark; doesn't apply to your boy at all. It was a detail that's been worrying me. On Mrs. Brooke's tack-room pad, when we looked at it after the murder, we found one sheet written in a child's hand, and the only thing we could be sure about was that it wasn't the same hand as any of the others' who left messages; so it seemed a reasonable conclusion that it might have been your boy's."

He paused interrogatively. Kit said impatiently, "There's no need for my children to use the pad. What did it say?"

"It said *The Killers are out again*. Can you think of any explanation of that?"

"Several."

"Imaginary games." Hobden was slowly nodding. "Not cowboys any longer, is it? Something from outer space seems to be the villain these days. Difficult when they're bright, I remember from when mine were young; they're so convincing you forget that they haven't quite the grasp on reality."

He stowed her bags away for her and left. Kit drove home revolving this opinion.

It was true enough as a working rule. The trouble seemed to her to lie in those disconcerting moments when her children grasped at imagination and found they had reality by the tail.

CHAPTER 12

"Please—please may I speak to Benjamin? It's Tracey Adams."

"He's out with the two-thirty, Tracey. Shall I get him to ring you?"

"No, I shan't be—we're going to the theatre, I don't know if I'll be able to—Mrs. Cullen, could you ask him to ring Jane? Jane Rolands. I'll leave the message with her. And as soon as he can, *please*."

Kit scribbled on the pad, adding, since the child sounded tense to the point of shaking, "I'll do my best, but I think he's going out with the four-thirty ride."

Tracey let out a moan of protest, hesitated, and said in a rush, "It's awfully important. Can you tell him, I've got the name. He'll understand."

She rang off quickly, and Kit scribbled again, wondering uneasily. As far as she knew, Benjamin had no friendly relations with what he called the Rolands lot; since they were all girls and around his own age, he despised them as much as they despised him. She made a point of seeing him when the two-thirty ride came in, calling across the mêlée in the yard, "Message for you on the pad." She heard the bell as he made a call, and a note of his voice, raised in excitement, or more likely, she thought, in exasperation. A moment later he skidded into the yard, dragged Lucy into a corner, and talked to her intensely for a moment. Lucy seemed to be objecting; Lucy was a sensible girl; Kit turned from weighing out tomatoes to call ominously, "Benjamin!"

He came scowling to her. She counted out change, bade her customer a smiling goodbye, and the instant she was gone wiped the smile off her face to snap, "What are you doing?"

"Nothing."

"Come on."

"Nothing. Going out with the ride."

"Go out with it, then. And straight back to supper."

He flung himself thunderously on Mouse and kicked him out of the yard, bullying anyone who got in his way.

Kit made a bad mistake. Being busy when the ride came in, she had time to look out only when the horses were in the home field. Mouse was there; so, she assumed, was Benjamin. She forgot that he had any number of accomplices who would lead a pony home for him, and if necessary do it unobserved.

In her usual way, Valentine had found herself a new piece of out-grazing, where at the corner of the council estate a derelict nursery had been sold to a newcomer, and there was a rough field to be grazed off. Lucy and Margaret took three horses up to Melcotts, and Jonty rode Gingerbread to the old nursery.

"I'm not too sure about the wire there," Valentine said, "but Gin's too lazy to break out. If you walk back I'll start the supper."

She needed, she noticed, more cheese. Walking leisurely up Hole Lane to the shop, which stayed open until

late, she saw Lucy in front of the freezer, and said play-
fully, "Boo."

Lucy swung round, stared, and burst into tears.

"But my dear stupid girl," said Valentine, distressed,
forgot the cheese, and gathered her up and took her
weeping to Hole Cottage. "What in heaven's name is the
matter? Sit down, have some coffee, stay to supper—yes,
of course stay to supper, I'll deal with your parents."

While Lucy sobbed, she telephoned her home. Her
mother showed no sign of awareness of trouble.

"Now what?" said Valentine to herself. She sat down
opposite Lucy and said, "You'd better snap out of that."

Lucy choked, "I'd promised Benjamin, that's why I did
it. But I felt terrible about it."

"Did what?"

"I said I'd do what I could, and he is right, isn't he, and
we should all do what we can to stop these Killers?"

Kit had not confided to Valentine Hobden's query
about the note on the tack-room pad. Valentine repeated
grimly, "Did what?"

"Gave him all the money I had. For a cab."

Valentine went back to the telephone.

"Kit—have you got your dear son?"

Kit began uncertainly, "Well, supper's a bit late—"

"You see if you can find your dear son. I'm on my way
with Lucy."

She wrote on her kitchen pad: *Jonty: nipped down to
Kit's, ham in frig, don't wait up*, bundled Lucy into her
van and drove her to Stumbletts. The kitchen was appe-
tizing with cheese toasting under the grill and Bridie was
expectantly in her place at table; but there was no Benjamin. Lucy took one look at Kit's white face, wailed,
"Oh, I feel so terrible," and put her head down on the
table and wept afresh.

Bridie looked unfathomably at the top of her head and said sweetly, "Can I have my supper, please?"

Kit ladled out cauliflower cheese, which for the next quarter of an hour Bridie ate slowly and steadily, her eyes turning from one speaker to the other and her spoon going from her plate to her mouth.

"Now, Lucy, come on," said Valentine.

"Where is my son?" said Kit.

"He's gone after the Killers, and I'm sure it's horribly dangerous, but Tracey saw the van again and got the name, and I gave him the money for a cab to get there, and I *told* him he shouldn't go by himself but you know what he is when he's set on something."

Bridie licked her spoon and said sweetly, "Yes, and he said he'd really get the Killers this time," and the telephone rang.

Kit went distractedly to answer it, and Valentine said to Bridie, "Lovey, who do you mean by the Killers?"

"Oh, don't you know?" said Bridie, looking covetously from her empty plate to the steaming dish. "It's what they call those horrible men who got Sheba. The meat-tin men who buy horses just to slaughter them for food, and not even proper slaughter with stunners and treating them well on the way there. Benjamin and all of us have been after them ever since they got Sheba."

The telephone said in Kit's ear, "That Mrs. Cullen? This is Mr. Tidy, Fred Tidy. Mrs. Brooke knows me, and my boy Chris comes up to your place to ride sometimes."

"I know Chris. And I know about you, Mr. Tidy. You helped one night when two of her ponies broke out."

"I did that," said Mr. Tidy's voice, "and very pleased, Mrs. Brooke being a neighbour of mine and been good to my boy. But those two ponies of hers, what I reckoned was that her real worry that night was the Killers. Am I right?"

After a pause Kit said, "I think you'd better talk to her yourself."

Valentine came quickly to the telephone, and after listening a moment said, "Take it that you're right, Mr. Tidy. And so?"

"And so you had a chestnut pony in that field across from my place, the old nursery that was. You haven't now."

"Gingerbread," said Valentine in anguish.

Lucy had stopped crying.

"It was after they got Sheba. We ought to have told you not to send that student with Chris and Benjamin, because Chris was always sending up his university airs, and Benjamin never got on with him anyway. And Benjamin told us afterwards, he went straight to look for Dave when they got there, and left Chris to help with Sheba, who never liked horse-boxes, you remember, and he had to wait while Dave finished his sale, and when they got back there was the student alone and this van pulling out of the gate. It had one corner bashed in at the back and the back window had been mended with wood so that you couldn't mistake it—Benjamin drew it for all of us afterwards so that we'd remember—and Dave was tall enough to see in and said there was a chestnut inside, but there was a crowd and they only ever saw the back of it."

"And I suppose," said Kit, very crisp though deathly pale, "that is what Tracey saw today?"

"Yes. They were going to the theatre at Chichester and stopped for lunch at the White Horse, and she saw it in the car park. So she slipped out to the telephone to let Benjamin know, though she had to do it through Jane Rolands, and Benjamin got me to give him all the money I had so that he could get a cab to go after them."

Before Kit could say anything, Valentine said, "Gingerbread has been stolen."

"So you see," Bridie said gently, "Benjamin was right after all, wasn't he? There was the name on the van. Belton Brothers, Station Approach, Stannisford. They're cattle dealers, it says in the directory."

"So you knew all about this too?" said Kit.

Bridie leant over to take a spoonful of cauliflower cheese from the dish and said, "Oh, yes, all of it. And I gave Benjamin the two pounds I had for my birthday."

Valentine put a quietening hand on Kit's arm. "Were you listening? Gingerbread's been stolen. Cattle dealers would have cattle-vans and lock-up sheds; the horse-meat trade is probably just a profitable by-line. They paid for Sheba; it wouldn't even all be illegal. But Gin's stolen, so we have the law on our side now. Where's Station Approach in Stannisford?"

Kit hit her forehead violently. "Left fork before you get to the Cattle Market. Wait—I remember; it's where the Cattle Market actually is. Station Approach must be those yards that back on to the market; the front's that shabby little row of shops, newsagent, greengrocer, a cheap furniture store; and there's an alley somewhere between them that leads into the market."

"That's the place. There'll be lock-up sheds in those yards. That's where Benjamin will be. And Gingerbread."

"And me," said Kit, reaching for her car keys.

"Wait. Yes, all right, that's where we'll all be, but we'll need more than us."

"Police," said Lucy. "You said, if Gin's been stolen—"

Valentine pulled a face. "He has. Unfortunately we only think we know who stole him. Wait, let me think; you have to have a warrant to search enclosed premises, don't you?—and presumably a sufficient reason for having the warrant. And it only needs a quick journey in that van to lose Gingerbread to us for good. . . . What we need here is some good shameless lying."

She went to the telephone and dialled three nines.

"Police, please. Mrs. Brooke of Hole Cottage. One of my ponies has been stolen, and it's of the greatest urgency to find him because I have reason to think that he is going for slaughter. Can you help me, please?"

"If you'll give us details, madam."

"The pony is a fourteen-two seven-year-old chestnut with a blaze and two white stockings, and was taken at some time after six this evening from the half-acre field belonging to the old nursery at the corner of the Hollow Cross estate. I believe the thieves were Belton Brothers of Station Approach, Stannisford."

The civil cautious voice said, "This is a serious allegation, Mrs. Brooke. Have you good reason for making it?"

"Very good indeed," said Valentine in her briskest voice. "I saw a van carrying their name and address coming from the direction of that field at seven-fifteen approximately this evening. This firm has already bought one of my horses for slaughter by giving a false name and address. I am on my way to Stannisford and I will go at once to the police station there. Will you notify them, please? Thank you." And she slapped down the receiver.

"You'll have some explaining to do later," said Kit, shaken. "And you didn't mention Benjamin."

"That's yours. Look, don't you see? What we've got to do is kick up all the fuss possible. Benjamin's in Stannisford looking for a stolen horse. What we need is the wrong conditions for lost boys and stolen horses—uproar; lights on, people knocked up, cops all over the place; and two lots of uproar is twice as useful as one."

"I get it. I'll take Dave; he's great at uproar."

"Yes, good. Don't make too much of Gingerbread to him; Dave wouldn't stir himself about a horse. Take your car down to his place, get him to ring the police, and ask him to drive you to Stannisford. Lucy, you stay and look after Bridie. Kit, all the torches you've got."

Bridie said in dulcet tones, "Benjamin stole my new torch."

"I'm glad he had that much sense." Valentine struggled into her coat. "I am waiting for Mr. Tidy to pick me up."

The name of Mrs. Brooke of Hole Cottage was familiar to the police by now, and after hesitation the desk sergeant rang Hobden at his home.

"Don't really know if you want to hear, sir, but we've had an emergency call from Mrs. Valentine Brooke: a stolen pony. It's not the Stumbletts murder, I think; just a case of the Killers."

"A case of the— Is that meant to make sense?"

"Sir? Killers; horses for illegal slaughter, you know. It's the common name."

"Well, for the love of heaven!" said Hobden. He went back to the supper-table and said to his wife, "Did you know that the horse-meat dealers are called Killers?"

"Of course I did," said she. "The regular dealers won't sell to them."

"No one thought of telling me," Hobden complained. He ate his apple charlotte, brooding on this new light. Stumbletts had lost one mare to the Killers; there had been that nervous chase along Church Lane that Elphick and Dickson had reported; obviously the children had taken the problem to heart. Was this a loose end in the murder ready to be tied up? The man at Stannisford was an old friend; when he had finished supper he rang him, looking for an amiable chat as well as a final note to append to his report.

Cornwell was not at home. "Dad got called out again," his daughter said crossly, "and he said something pretty rude about you as he went. What have you done to him?"

What indeed? And why should Cornwell be called out for a missing horse? Hobden rang Stannisford station.

"Horse? I don't know anything about a horse," Cornwell said. "A boy I'm after, from somewhere over your way. Why can't you keep your boys out of my free evenings?"

"Wouldn't by any chance be a boy called Cullen?"

Luckier than Cornwell, Hobden had had his supper; and it was a fine evening and he did not want to mow the lawn, and it would be nice to get a line on what that poor girl had been doing at the stables. He took out his car keys.

As Valentine emerged from the Stumbletts gate, there was the clang of a bicycle dropped to the ground, and Jonty leaped from the darkness to her side.

"Caught you. *Get* whoever stole Gin. Mark rang me," she said, breathing hard.

"*Mark?*"

Mr. Tidy's rattling old van drew up by them with a waft of fish, and the door swung open for Valentine. Voices called Jonty from within, and she sprang round to the back to dive in there.

"You got young Jonty," said Mr. Tidy with approval as he leant over to slam the door. "Dunno quite who I got, but they seemed to sprout from the ground the moment the young gent shouted *Gingerbread.*" He let in his clutch with a flying jolt.

"Young gent?" said Valentine, turning to peer into the back, where groans and curses marked the passengers' efforts to sit tight.

"Mark, of course," said a chorus.

"How did Mark get into this act?"

"I saw Jonty putting him in the field," said Mark's shy

voice from the darkness, "and when I took him down an apple he'd gone. And I remembered Mr. Tidy from the other night, and he was nearer than my telephone."

"And he insisted on ringing young Jonty and young Margaret, and my Chris isn't in but young Colin had come down for some fish so he nipped in too. Got any more troops back there?"

"No," said the chorus, and Colin's slow voice added, "Chris'll be mad to miss this."

Mr. Tidy changed down tearingly for the turn, snarled round it, and got into top gear and top speed again in a series of frenetic jerks. "Not a chicken, the old van, but she'll make it!" he shouted above the noise.

Someone called from the back, "What do we do then?"

Valentine waited for a little calm to brief her troops. "What you have to remember," she said with all the emphasis she could muster, "is that we are in the right, legal, and approved by the fuzz. If anything frightens you, open your mouth and shriek blind bloody murder, and you'll be all right. Got that?"

"Got that."

But the trouble with this lot, she saw, was that it was going to be difficult to get them sensibly frightened.

"This bloody little nephew of mine," said Dave Cullen, cursing oncoming headlights that did not dip for him on the outskirts of Stannisford: "what do you reckon the little bugger will have been up to all this time? Looking for that flat-footed chestnut?"

"Dave, you haven't been listening," said Kit tiredly. Dave would have defended his brother's boy from the wrath of God if necessary, but it took time to get an idea into his head, and anyway he would have his retribution for an interrupted evening. "Benjamin doesn't know that Gingerbread's been stolen."

"Just be swanning around looking for horses in general, then?"

"Not horses in general: horses locked up in hiding. And for Belton Brothers." Kit leant forward as the street-lighting of Stannisford sprang up around them. "It's somewhere near here, a left fork to the Cattle Market."

"Horses hidden on the premises of Belton Brothers." Dave coasted deliberately past the turn and pulled in at the pavement.

"Dave, that's the turn. Back up, can't you?"

"Ah, that's the turn." Dave slid from his seat and slammed the door behind him. "Move over, girl. Police station's somewhere up there and turn right; you'll find it."

"I will not." Kit dived for the door and found him holding it against her.

"Don't be bloody silly, girl. The silly little sod's looking into Killers' nasty secrets, and those lads can be rough. I'll nip down first and have a nose around."

Mr. Tidy snapped off his lights and edged the van to a halt just outside the high scaffolding gate with CATTLE MARKET on its crossbar.

"Lights still up," he said with a glance at his watch, "but I think they douse at midnight, so let's have a good look while we can."

The few high overhead lights shone on a broad expanse of rough ground, divided by iron rails. At the lower end a track led to the railway yard; on the two sides above, untidy fences in various states of repair divided the market from buildings with long backyards behind them.

"There!" said the chorus behind her, subdued now by excitement. "There, Val, look: there are sheds in most of those yards, all kinds of sheds. That's where Gin'll be."

There were a lot of the yards; and at that moment the lights went out.

There were scrambling noises at the back of the van, and Valentine said at once, "Not yet. You won't be able to see. Count to a hundred and then get out. Come on, Mr. Tidy."

They got out. "Case we need to chase," said Mr. Tidy, and left the keys in the ignition lock. "Lots of sheds," he said, depressed.

"Did you see any names up?"

"Didn't seem to have them. This pony of yours: I've seen you catching them mornings. You've got a sort of whistle. That be any help?"

Valentine hesitated. "Gingerbread would recognize it; but he'll be tied up. Well, he'll shift about. We'll have to depend on our ears, Mr. Tidy, and that means getting up close to all those sheds, one by one."

"Ah," said Mr. Tidy. He added after thought, "And dead quiet too. If they hear us and suspect, they might try to smuggle him away. That case, back to the van and hang on to them."

"Right. You hear, you lot?"

"Yes, Val." They had emerged, all swinging torches. "But we can't do your whistle, Val. The horses know it isn't you."

"Try. He'll be unsettled. Now, quiet as we can, because some of those houses will be occupied, and we don't want to be held up as burglars at one end while they're whisking Gin away at the other. Half of you with Mr. Tidy to the left, half with me to the right, and we'll work round and meet in the middle. See you."

"See you." The dim figures melted into the darkness, with them a blur that she recognized as Jonty's matelot shirt. Good girl; she knew more about the horses than any of the others. "Who's staying with me?"

"Margaret and Mark, Val."

It was Colin with Jonty then: a slow boy, but steady.

They felt their way under rails and came up against the first of the fences.

They had looked rickety, but nevertheless they were six-foot screens, and the gates were locked and bolted, top and bottom by the feel when she put her shoulder against them. Mark was the lightest; he bent his knee and Margaret heaved him up until he could get his elbows over the fence; Valentine came to his other side and took half his weight. He was a diffident boy and a nervous rider, but apparently had the makings of a very fair burglar; he hung there calmly and took his time before he slid down.

"No. Garden-type shed, door too small for a pony, and an open shelter with piles of packing-cases."

They moved on to the next, and put him up. Almost at once he whispered down, "Val, whistle, will you?"

Come and be caught! Valentine chirruped.

They strained their ears. All that Valentine could hear was Margaret's breath catching with the strain of Mark's weight on her shoulder.

Mark down again. "No. Big shed enough, but broken windows this side. We'd have heard hooves easily."

Next yard. They felt the sag of Mark's dismay. "Big new shed. Windows don't open. Wait." He squirmed along the top of the fence and tipped perilously over the gate. Coming down with a rush and gasping at a scraped elbow, he said, "Padlocked. But there are hay-bales everywhere."

Valentine crooked her knee and said to Margaret, "Give me a bunt up."

"You'll never get back," said Margaret, taking fright.

"Hay-bales." Valentine got a knee over the fence and sat boldly astride. The yard was long and narrow and cluttered; the big shed on the right, on the left the high white wall of the next-door building; the house at the far end was tall and narrow. She was on the point of swinging her other leg over and dropping into the yard when some movement caught her eye.

Now what movement could she have seen in the darkness? Only light: a very dim swath of light through a high window in the narrow house. Dim, and fleeting too: a torch behind a window.

A scrabbling below made her hiss down, "No, keep quiet."

"An oil drum. I can get up by myself."

"Not yet. And be quiet."

She kept her eyes steadily on the house. House?—no, the window where she had seen the light had been uncurtained. Premises behind and above a tiny shop, then, let off with the yard as storage space.

There was the light again. Given the perspective, she saw that at her first glimpse it had been in a second-storey window; now it had come down a flight; the note of a voice floated out, at conversational pitch; the torchlight vanished, and then an unshaded electric bulb was lit on the ground floor.

Searching, thought Valentine, suddenly hopeful: searching with a torch upstairs. A man's figure crossed the light, was joined by another, and both moved away. She whispered over the wall, "Mark, get Mr. Tidy," and swinging her leg over dropped softly into the yard. She was promptly nearly killed by Margaret's dropping on top of her.

"Who told you to come, blast you?"

"You can't get back alone. Look, the hay-bales."

They were experts with hay-bales; they had three at the bottom of the wall, securing their retreat, in a couple of silent moments. The light in the bottom room was still on, but both men had vanished. Valentine stopped to prospect.

The shed, built of cement panels, had a vented roof; the windows would not need to open. Margaret was doing something around its nearer end. Between its farther end and the house was an untidy patch, difficult to make out in that light, lean-to shelters and stacked rubbish. Could a boy be hiding there?

The thought had only entered her head when the house-door opened and the figure of a man was outlined against the light.

He was a broad-shouldered man who was going bald; she could see clearly the dip in the line of his shaggy hair. He was talking over his shoulder to someone in the room behind him; it sounded like the exasperated snap at the end of a long disagreement. He had a torch; Valentine pulled back as he switched it on, and cast a worried glance to be sure Margaret was not in its line. The beam swung idly for a moment and then fastened on the rubbish beside the door.

No, no boy there: a wheelbarrow, a pile of tyres, half a dozen petrol-cans. The torch was switched off and the door shut. If they were looking for a boy, it seemed as if they had not found one. She saw that Margaret was working on the hay-bales, building one on another in the hope of reaching a window; she had started to her help when a powerful new light sprang out on her left.

It illumined the whole breadth of the yard, cutting her off from Margaret and the shed, and its back-glow threw her own shadow on to the wall. She fell back against the only camouflage possible, an iron ladder running all the way up the wall. The light came from a window in the wall; of course; it was not a wall, it was a building, a flat-roofed building, and this ladder led to the roof. Up on the roof would be the safest spot, if the two men were going to search the building, but Margaret could not cross the yard and she could not leave her.

She had a pile of bales below the window now, and was slowly pulling herself upright on them.

And a step sounded behind Valentine, and a torch-beam fixed on her.

It just missed Margaret, who ducked and toppled. Valentine stepped straight into it to hide her, smiling and saying, "Oh, there *is* someone there!" while she wondered where it had come from. There must be a rear door to this building; and as she pictured the long single-storey building with windows along the side she realized what it was. There was a furniture-shop in the street outside, a gimcrack frontage with a triangular false pediment high above it to give the effect of a pitched roof at the least possible expense.

"Didn't think there would be, did you?" said an angry voice. "What do you think you're doing here?"

"Looking for you, I think," Valentine said cheerily. "Would you be one of the Belton brothers?"

"None of your business," said the man, coming closer. He held the light on her, but in its dim reflection she could see a lean wiry face with a drooping moustache, a knotty forearm, and very dusty knees to his trousers; he must have been searching for Benjamin under all the furniture in the store. "I own this yard and you're trespassing. How did you get in?—jemmy the gate?"

"Burgled it," Valentine agreed blithely. "Better call the police, hadn't you?"

"I don't need the fuzz to look after my own," said the man. He stepped very close, and she could not retreat for fear of turning the torch-beam towards Margaret. As he caught at her arm she side-stepped him away from the shed, turning him with his back to it. Over his shoulder she saw Margaret, once more balanced on her pile of hay-bales, lift something heavy in one hand and strike it hard against the window above her head.

The window exploded and smashed with a startling noise. The man swung round from her with an exclamation, and through the broken window came the sound of shifting hooves.

Valentine put two fingers in her mouth and let out her *achtung* whistle. The hooves plunged. Margaret, who had brought herself to her knees by the energy of her swing, shrieked at the top of her voice, "Gingerbread, my Gingerbread!" and from the Cattle Market came an assortment of shrieks and calls as Mr. Tidy and his party scrambled their way across. "On our way! Quick! Hold on, Val, we're coming."

And over it all a powerful voice from the other side of the furniture store shouted, "Benjamin lad, I see you!"

The torch went out and the Belton brother vanished. Someone beyond the wall screamed, "The roof, the roof!" Valentine pulled herself up the ladder and pelted across the roof.

From ground level on the other side a powerful light was holding steady on the very tip of the false pediment. It rose twenty feet above the roof, a single screen of brick edged with thin slabs of stone rising at an angle of forty-five degrees. At its tip a small bundle of rags was clinging immobile.

"Oh my God," said Valentine, appalled.

There were no handholds, no footholds except the thin division between slabs. He must have gone up an inch at a time, pulling himself by fingertips and straddled knees. Only extreme fear could have sent him up there. Extreme fear, this time of falling, was holding him there, head down, knees up, hands bunched, unable to move.

Valentine shouted into the darkness, "Lights up here!" Mark swarmed up the ladder and added the beam of his torch to Dave's; Jonty followed him; Mr. Tidy's voice could be heard organizing them, and from the other side Dave's powerful bellow asked, "How the hell do I get up there?"

The two torches steadied on the small hands. The fingers were flat and clawed, strained to their utmost. Valentine ran to the far side and shouted, "Dave, don't try to get up. We need ladders, fire-brigade."

"Oke," assented Dave's voice, already receding.

"Time?" said Jonty's calm voice as she came back. "He's stuck. Slipped already."

"Hay-bales," said Mark, springing away. They were already being bundled up the ladder; Jonty went to help.

It meant a heave to the foot of the ladder; two heaves up to the roof; a staggering rush across the roof. How many bales to make a safe landing for a child stiff with terror?

And if he fell the other way?

There was a siren in the street below.

"Fire-engine?"

Jonty was leaning over the edge. "No. Police."

"Pray heaven Kit isn't anywhere here."

"That hand. I think he's going—"

And bouncing confident footsteps danced across the roof towards them, and a bouncing confident voice called, "Half a sec, Benj boyo, and I'm with you!"

Valentine turned her head; she could suddenly hardly move. By her side was a small skinny figure, struggling out of a jacket, kicking off shoes. It rose once or twice on bare arching toes, shook its shoulders lightly, stretched and flexed wrists and fingers. Head tipped back to look up, it called, "On my way, Benj!" and was.

"Monkey!" breathed Jonty.

He put fingers and toes to the edges of the pediment, seeming to grip with all four equally easily. He kept the curve of his body clear of the stone, balancing himself delicately between friction and gravity, between hands pulling up and toes pulling down, and calmly walked up to Benjamin.

Benjamin's hand had lost its hold; it fell nerveless. Gently, in mid-air on his toes, Chris's hands went slowly down on to Benjamin's, brought it back to its hold. His cracking voice said conversationally, "Bloody nasty old spot this, boy, shall us nip down?" He set the clutching hands firm, inched down the knees, slid down the hands, inched down the knees; and just once, at the very last, the moment before Valentine and Mr. Tidy could catch him and swing him to safety, Benjamin moved his own hands down.

The skinny figure on the pediment, unbelievably, rose to its full height, threw up its arms, and jumped. Valentine bit on her impulse to shriek. The figure did a forward roll, bounced lithely to its feet, and came towards them grinning. Skinny little Chris, smudged with dirt from the pediment, fingers smudged with blood, was all one glow as they swarmed on to the roof, Margaret, Mark, Colin, Dave at last finding his way up, a strange policeman taking charge, all surrounding him. But the chief glow was from Mr. Tidy, who dumped Benjamin on to Valentine and seized his son's hands.

"Hi, dad," said Chris.

"Not bad, son," said Mr. Tidy.

Valentine had Benjamin, and Jonty was helping her get him down from the roof. "I can manage him," she said. "Go and find Kit first, that's all; just find Kit."

Thankfully, once she had found Kit and restored to her her son, she gave up trying to keep abreast of everything that was happening. She noted Margaret and Jonty with Gingerbread, Margaret weeping happy tears on his neck, and then assented to the suggestion of some policemen that she should go back with them to the station and explain things. There they insisted on giving her strong tea with sugar in it, which she disliked, and she was humiliated to find that she was content to hand over to Dave Cullen the explaining. He did not get any of it wrong, she noted, but he told it as he had seen it, which made it seem rather different; she assented to it all without correction. It did not matter, now that they had Benjamin back and Gingerbread safe.

"And those Belton brothers?" she found a moment to ask.

"Scarpered," the police told her with little regret. "Not to worry, Mrs. Brooke, we'll pick them up very quickly. There were a couple more horses in with yours, which must please you. Of course we'll need a—"

"Witness statement," she nodded gently; and suddenly found herself looking at Hobden.

"Must be getting good at statements, Mrs. Brooke," he said.

"Good heavens, Mr. Hobden. But isn't this Stannisford? What are you doing here?"

"Here on your account, I'm afraid."

"You can't possibly—" Valentine pulled herself up in her chair and put down the teacup that had sagged sideways in her hand. "I'm sorry, I was almost asleep. You can't possibly think that this has anything to do with Jill's death or Brian's."

Hobden nodded at the sergeant, who gave him his chair and went out. "I can, you know, ma'am. Mrs. Cullen didn't tell you about the message on the tack-room pad? It seems that young Benjamin had organized all your young riders to look out for the Killers. I take it that he wouldn't have omitted Jill?"

Valentine thought about it. "No. He wouldn't have omitted Jill."

"So, contrary to what you supposed, Jill would have had reason to be worried about the cream—and about your other horses. Anything at all might have aroused her suspicions—strangers about the place, meetings late at night, a strange Range Rover that could have been used to tow a horse-box. Cantrell and his friends wouldn't have been stupid enough to try to meet actually in Stumbletts, but anywhere nearby—"

"Yes, I see," said Valentine. "Would there be a cigarette anywhere around here, do you think?" He found her one, and she lay back in her chair and smoked in silence for a time. At last she said, "Kids. Jill goes haring off after strangers because she thinks they are after her horse, and gets herself killed. Benjamin does the same thing, and—Am I putting it too high?"

"The Beltons aren't in the same class as the lot who knocked off Cantrell. But still nasty to handle. The boy wasn't stupid to take a risk in hiding from them."

"Thank you. I'll tell him that if I may; it ought to please him." She got up stiffly. "I came in Mr. Tidy's van; did I hear that he'd taken the children home?"

"And Mr. Cullen has taken his sister-in-law and the boy. I asked them to keep you until we could have a word. I'll get a car to take you home."

"That would be kind. I suppose we say goodbye for good now."

He took the hand she held out, but said, "I'm afraid we'll have to meet when it comes to court, Mrs. Brooke."

"Oh, yes, but that will be different. I meant—well, I'm not sure really what I did mean, I think. Sorry, but I seem to be rather tired."

But she knew very well what she meant.

In the police-car taking her home, she sat in the back and thought.

Chris, Chris Tidy: son of that nice Mr. Tidy. No one remembered his mother, who had left the home long ago.

There had been a grandmother Tidy who had kept house at first, and then declined into senility and finally died. Now father and son lived alone in the council house. Until he had drifted to the stables, Chris had hung round in the holidays while his father was at work; once or twice he had been cautioned for shop-lifting, though no one had the heart to upset his father by prosecuting. At school he had risen a little above the rest by proving himself a natural gymnast; but where had that led him?

Only, really, to the rescue of Benjamin tonight.

Riding had been a disappointment to him, she had seen. He had hoped to rise above the rest again, but had failed. Even the younger riders had scorned him. Jill especially had scorned him.

Chris had gone with Benjamin and the student to sell Sheba. Chris and Benjamin both had been instructed to go to find Dave; but only Benjamin had gone. And the Killers had arrived to buy Sheba within minutes.

Chris had not gone with them to Stannisford tonight. Chris had been out somewhere when Mark had raised the alarm. Gingerbread had been stolen from the field opposite Chris's home after Chris had gone out. Chris had appeared in the Beltons' yard to rescue Benjamin the moment it had become clear that the Beltons had decamped.

Yes, but Chris had rescued Benjamin.

Funny: perhaps Hobden was in the right of it after all, and Jill really had gone to Stumbletts because she suspected Chris of being one of the Killers. Yes, that was very likely. Nothing else would have roused in Jill such contempt that it had to be met by that first blow with the horseshoe, that blow from which there could be no retreat.

And Chris *had* rescued Benjamin; and there was his father, that nice Mr. Tidy, to be thought of.

Yes; it was goodbye for good to Hobden.

CHAPTER 13

To Valentine's deep relief, Mr. Tidy called on her next day to tell her that he was taking Chris with him on a visit to his brother in Hastings. "It's the fishing," he explained. "Went in July when I had a couple of days off, and Chris took to the fishing. We'll bring you back a good parcel of herring."

That explained where the blood-stained clothes had gone. Sadly, she was glad to see the back of Mr. Tidy.

They could not leave the small stable empty, a constant reminder of Jill, and they did not care to use it as it had been. On one rest-day, working from dawn to dusk, they whitewashed it inside and out, moved in the saddle-racks and polish-shelf, called it the tack-room, and put a blind across the window of the old tack-room and a row of hooks and a mirror on the wall and called it the changing-room. Valentine tore her forearm on a rusty nail during the painting, put some strapping on it, and pulled it off impatiently when it failed to stick.

Diana took Azul to his first show in the middle of August. Jonty had been working hard on him, and he behaved impeccably. Diana grew a little above herself and

took him into the clear-round jumping, where she inter-
fered with his mouth so much that after the second jump
he delivered himself of a couple of irritated bucks. Diana
came off and lay groaning on the grass.

"Fake groans," said Kit uncharitably, when the plump-
faced fiancé had taken the girl tenderly off.

"She was winded."

"If you ask me, Azul will be for sale this evening. What
are you going to do about it?"

"Butter," said Valentine, and went to see Diana's father. Before the show was over she had not only swapped
Azul for Snowgoose but sold Fox to a complete stranger
who happened to be talking to the Aubreys, and had a little more to put towards the price of the winter feed.
Amanda, whose grandmother had hired her big Robert
for the day, and was too overhorsed for comfort, and
Tracey, who had a Best Rider rosette on Justin, came tear-
ing over to her shouting, "Someone said we've got Fallada
back!"

"Who?"

"The blue-eyed cream."

"Azul has been with us all the time."

"Yes, but that Diana would go on about *my* horse, and
ride him like a dripping hen." Tracey did a wounding impression of Diana, who had not yet learnt to keep her
elbows in. "Is he ours again?"

"All right, he's ours again. What is this name you will
all call him?"

Tracey had cantered off cheering. The stolid Amanda,
thumping heels on Robert's ribs to move him from his
own sedate pace, said between kicks, "Grimm's Fairy
Tales."

"What?"

"*Princess, princess, if thy mother could see thee now!*"
Robert got under way and carried her off, leaving Val-

entine, sobered, to assemble her memories of the story. Not a nice one, even by the Brothers Grimm's standards. The wicked stepmother had nailed the dead horse's head above the archway, and as the girl trudged beneath she had said, *O Fallada, Fallada, if my mother could see me now!*

The next day she found the *Azul* label on the saddle-rack removed and a neat *Fallada* substituted. They did not see Diana for some time, but when she did come she shamed them for their lack of charity by noticing all Snowgoose's good points.

Not very long after this show, Kit noted that Valentine had a bandage on her arm, and was tendering it as she worked. She took hold to look more closely, and Valentine shied violently.

Round the plaster the arm was hot and puffy. "Is that where you snagged it when we were changing the tack-room? Looks as if it could do with an antibiotic shot."

"Haven't time. Don't fuss."

That night Jonty telephoned Kit from Hole Cottage. "I think Val's gone nuts or something. She won't sit down and she won't eat and she keeps talking nonsense."

"What sort of nonsense?"

"Archways and stepmothers. And I think she must have a temperature."

"I bet she must," said Kit. "Get the doctor along, Jonty. Don't ask her, just get him."

Valentine was in bed for two days on antibiotics, and back at the stables on the third, against orders, her belt a hole tighter and apt to sit down suddenly on hay-bales. When Kit tried to make her rest, they quarrelled violently. At her wits' end, Kit summoned Caspar for the week-end; and Caspar dealt with her firmly.

"Mamma, please be quiet. You are working yourself to death. Why?"

"I'm missing Jill," Valentine said mulishly.

"And will continue to miss her. How many horses have you?"

"Well: twenty-seven."

"Twenty-seven?"

"They crept up on me. I had two for selling on, and they'll make twice their purchase price when they're schooled, but I haven't had time for that. And then the Gaines children had outgrown their two, and let me have them for practically nothing because they wanted to be sure they'd have a good home—"

"You still have to feed them."

"Yes, but they're nice ponies and will be just right for beginners next summer."

"Mamma," said Caspar patiently, "this is *this* summer."

He stayed another ten days, and by the end of it the stable was considerably trimmed and he had quarrelled with his mother half a dozen times. He knew better than to look for buyers for Gingerbread, Robert, Justin, or any of the other ponies she had had for years, but he disposed of half a dozen of those she had less sentiment for, and Kit saved him from the disaster of laying a finger on Fallada. For the rest of the time he worked on the sellers-on. He saw no point in riding, but was a meticulous and merciless schooler, and achieved a triumph by selling three at once to a large and expensive riding-school ten miles away, and if the price did not entirely come up to his figures he knew his mamma too well to say so. They parted on their usual affectionate terms.

"And you know," Valentine said to Kit, "he almost seemed to be enjoying himself towards the end. Maybe he's fonder of riding than we thought."

My dear Mamma, Caspar wrote in his next letter: *I hope your arm is quite recovered and you yourself finding your work less wearing.*

"Pompous boy," said Valentine; and replied: *My arm is perfectly all right. As for the stable, the autumn term has begun so it's only the week-ends that are full. I was offered a beautiful 15.2½TB 4-yr-old who would have been just what I wanted for adult rides next year, but refused him.* This was not wholly true, as the offer had been tentative and she had wrung out an assurance that the fifteen-two-hander could be hers for the asking in the spring; but she felt that if Caspar was going to take to bullying her she owed it to herself to keep him guessing. Caspar suspected that this was in her mind, but could not be sure, which made their relations normal and cordial. He wrote back: *My dear Mamma: Would it be convenient if I were to come down for the week-end of November 28th? I would very much like also to bring a friend with me. I know you have only the one spare room, and she would like to stay with you, so could I ask you to find me somewhere to sleep for that week-end?*

Never before had Caspar had a girl he chose to introduce to her, let alone bring for a week-end. In as much of a flutter as if it had been her own first love, Valentine took the letter with her to Stumbletts.

"Good heavens," said Kit, "but does she ride?"

"He doesn't say."

"Oh, *men.* He surely wouldn't bring her for your busy time unless she did. He can have my spare room."

Valentine rang Caspar in the evening. He sounded detached, which meant that he was not. "Bed at Stumbletts? That is most kind of Mrs. Cullen; I shall enjoy that. Ride?—but of course Diana rides. Mamma, what are you thinking of? You taught her yourself."

"Diana? Not Diana Aubrey?"

"Didn't I mention her name?"

Valentine said warmly, "No, you did not, and you know it. The last time I heard of Diana Aubrey she was

formally engaged to someone else and you were supposed
to be schooling my horses."

"Well, formal engagements," Caspar said dismissively.
"And you are quite mistaken, Mamma. I was devotedly
schooling your horses. You forget that Diana and I are
very old friends."

They must have been meeting in London, thought Valentine, and now she chooses Hole Cottage rather than her
parents' house to stay in. Deeply impressed, she began to
throw herself into a panic about food and drink.

"For the love of God," said Kit in disgust, "a week ago
you'd have given her bread and cheese at the kitchen
table. Much more to the point, what rides have you got
over the week-end? Jonty and I could take them if you
want to stay with Caspar and his intended."

"No!" said Valentine in a panic. "They won't want
that. I wouldn't want that. I'll take the rides as usual.
Nothing in the afternoons but the old faithfuls."

In these cold months, only the hardy children came
regularly, and there was time for only one afternoon ride,
so that the out-grazers had to be taken at two-thirty.

"Saturday afternoon: Robert, Gingerbread, Harvey,
and Sailor to go to Melcotts, and only Margaret and Lucy
and the Rolands girls booked in. Benjamin and Bridie
coming too? Diana will want her Snowgoose, and Caspar
goes well on Ebony; that will leave Barnaby for me and
Fallada for Jonty."

"Diana won't have happy memories of Fallada."

"Then she'll have to stand them," Valentine said re-
freshingly. "Jonty likes him and he needs exercise." She
lapsed pitiably by adding, "And if I could borrow your
chicken-brick—"

Kit snorted her contempt. But she lent the chicken-
brick, and supplied tarragon, and put chrysanthemums in
her spare room for Caspar on Friday evening. He arrived

at the correct hour of six-forty, presented her with a correct bottle of good sherry, and occupied the bathroom for ten minutes before taking himself off to Hole Cottage.

"He won't," said Benjamin, "he *can't*. Not a girl with hands like that."

"I think he will," Bridie observed gently.

Helping tack up for the first ride next morning, Kit murmured to Valentine, "How did it go last night?"

"The chicken was all right, and Caspar'd brought enough wine for a dozen banquets. But, Kit, the girl's *impossible*. She just sits there, radiating her conviction that he couldn't be improved."

"It's a free country."

"It would be the ruin of him."

Caspar and Diana turned up together for the two-thirty ride. They both wore cream jodhpurs, cashmere sweaters, and tweed jackets, and Kit had to take refuge behind a girthing to hide her tendency to giggle at Valentine's face. A little later Valentine came behind her and muttered savagely, "You wait till Benjamin brings home his first girl-friend!"

For late November it was a pleasant day, mild and open, the trees not yet stripped of all their leaves, the going underfoot soft but not miry. "Ride herd, Jonty!" Valentine called, and led the way on Barnaby. Ebony and Snowgoose filed through the gate after her, and Benjamin and Bridie crowded squabbling behind. Jonty, already up on Fallada, called tolerantly into the big stable, "You lazy lot ready yet?" and raised her broad bee-stung brows to Kit.

"Out-grazers?" Kit asked idly.

"No problem. We'll get left behind!" she shouted into the stable, and ducking her head walked Fallada under the door. "See you," she added over her shoulder.

"Have a good ride." Kit snapped her fingers for Dandy

and went into the kitchen to start her week's baking. Horses clattered by at the trot as she put the flour-jar on the table, and she saw the two Rolands girls riding grimly by. Leaning to the window to be sure they had closed the gate after them, she saw that they were not the last; Robert and Gingerbread were after them, Jonty was leaning from Fallada to pull the gate to, and in front of her the rump of the big grey Harvey obscured some smaller horse at his side.

What smaller horse?

Of course; Valentine had mentioned Sailor among the out-grazers.

Counting tablespoons of flour into the scale, in another part of her mind she automatically checked over the riders. That was Mark on Harvey, and Margaret and Lucy would of course be on their favourites Gingerbread and Robert.

Then who was that on Sailor?

Some reliable rider booked in late. But the silhouette of the rider, only momentarily seen behind Harvey, stayed in her mind with a troubling persistence. Small, skinny, riding rather too short as if he had ambitions to be a jockey: surely it was Chris?

Nothing had been seen of Chris since he had gone on holiday in the summer. The boy who rescued Benjamin, and she had not spoken to him? Kit ran to the door to look out.

But the ride had vanished on to the common; it was too late. Kit went slowly back to her baking. Chris: they had heard that he had got a job in Hastings. Or had they assumed it, because he had vanished from Hollow Cross, though Mr. Tidy was still in his shabby little house? She could not remember. All the year's stable-lads had gone, with the exception of Mark, just as they always went at the end of the summer.

Valentine could not have known he was here. He must have come in late. He must have strolled in late, when Jonty was hurrying on the out-grazers.

Diana was an idiot and would be bad for Caspar, but otherwise had genuine charm, Valentine had to acknowledge as they rode through the woods. In his presence she rode more nervously than ever, but she was grateful for Snowgoose's care of her, and was at least discovering how to keep her hands down and her elbows in. Caspar led the three of them up the long ride they called the gallop, holding Ebony to a moderate trot, and at the top they halted to wait for the others. Jonty sent them up in pairs, for the ride was narrow. Benjamin on fiery little Mouse arrived at a gallop and was carried far beyond them, Bridie on Cupid at a neat canter pulling up precisely at Valentine's side, and the Rolands girls side by side, each telling the other to get out of her way. Then Mark came up alone on Harvey, rolling a little but surprisingly secure bareback, and said, "Jonty says okay, not to wait."

"Yes, no need to watch over the others. It's going to get chilly as the sun goes down. What about the old road, so that we can warm up with a good canter?"

Diana went enormous-eyed and fearful. Caspar said firmly, "That would be very nice, Mamma," and pulled Ebony around beside Snowgoose. Valentine, dolefully feeling that her sympathies were turning towards Diana, fell back to the young ones and issued some admonitions.

"If you lose one stirrup, Karen, don't weave around feeling for it, lose the other. And, Jane, you *must* shorten your rein, or you'll be jinked over half the county. Watch Jonty now. She's always in touch with her horse's mouth but never interfering."

Fallada came beautifully up the ride, and Jane let out a moan of envy.

"Yes, she's brought him on well," Valentine approved. "Who else have you got down there, Jonty?"

Jonty looked serene, her cheeks pink, her lips lifting into their faint smile. "Dunno quite who, really. Lucy and Margaret are bringing them up. Old road and a canter?"

"We'll go on." Valentine was trying to steer the narrow path between neglecting Caspar and Diana and burdening them with her company. "You lot come behind us." She bustled Barnaby through the gaps that led to the steep slope up to the old road. Diana was riding half a length behind Caspar, thumping her saddle in sheer nervousness at the sight of his repellently correct trot.

"He's such a marvellous rider," she confided breathlessly. "I shall never be anything like him."

"Oh yes you will," said Valentine, suddenly making up her mind to it in sheer dislike of her son. "Stop looking at him, it's got you out of synch with 'Goose. Sit hard, let her take you. *Stop* looking at Caspar. Good, your hands are very good now. Now—rise, not much, up-down, you'll get it easily if you feel her trot." Sweet-tempered Snowgoose, used to novices, pounded her way along the straight track without a check, and in a few minutes Diana had her head up and a smile on her face.

One of these days, Valentine silently told her son, I'm going to put her up against you, on a better horse, and see that she *wins*.

And Caspar was riding again. Perhaps this situation was not as bad as she had feared.

The old road here was embanked well above the level of the surrounding fields. It was a pleasant place for a ride, with the great coverts of dog-rose at either side now brilliant with hips and hung with drifts of old-man's beard. Already at the other side of the fields, where the river ran, a thin veil of mist was rising.

Ahead of them was Hugletts Bridge, where the road

lifted over the new farm road below. Valentine looked
behind at the rest of her ride bucketing happily in the
road, and said quietly to Diana, "Shorten your rein and
sit down hard. Now, 'Goose!'" She clucked the mare and
Barnaby to a canter. They overtook the unaware Caspar,
Diana letting out a small gasp at the change of pace but
not quite grabbing for the mane, and in a spurt of thirty
yards beat him to the bridge.

Valentine took Barnaby in a wide turn to give Diana
her triumph alone, and trotted back to them in time to see
Diana lying forward to embrace Snowgoose and Caspar
looking at her. At the sight of his face she looked hur-
riedly elsewhere, thinking, "Yes, it's my daughter-in-law
all right. Maybe there is something in her that I haven't
seen yet."

"Give the young ones room," she said, taking Barnaby
to the left-hand verge and turning him to watch. Surprisingly the young ones—Jane and Karen, Benjamin and Bridie—were riding fast but seriously, not even Benjamin at-
tempting to bully anyone. "Enjoy that?" she asked, and
they said obediently, "Yes, thank you, Val," without any
of the usual arguing about who had gone faster than
whom.

The older ones, on the other hand, were noticeably
noisier than usual, as if there had been horseplay farther
back. It did not matter; they were all capable—even Mark
was showing confidence today—and Jonty had them well
in hand. They seemed to have been practising riding
without reins, an exercise she encouraged on this wide
level track; Jonty came up at a very fast canter, her reins
knotted on Fallada's neck, her whip in both hands high
above her head. The rest followed her, mostly with their
hands lower and ready to catch the reins, and with
shrieks of laughter scattered among the gorse coverts on
the right of the track. Four bareback riders, she noted au-

tomatically, right for the out-grazers; but before she could check them among the gorse Jonty trotted up to her, faintly smiling, round cheeks only a little pinker than usual.

Diana said laughing, "Jonty and Fallada, you're both lovely!" Jonty looked at her under the broad bee-stung brows and went a little redder.

"Val, we've time for the jumps."

Valentine looked at her watch. "Yes, we came fast so we're early. Not too long, the light's going."

Jonty nodded and took Fallada across the road to organize the line. Caspar asked in surprise, "Jumps?"

"Do you want to try? That line of cement blocks over on the other side. A bit unorthodox, but useful. They rebuilt the bridge higher last season, and left a pile of broken blocks; so we rolled and heaved them into a miniature course. No height, of course—even beginners can hop across on the smallest pony, but it teaches them to judge their take-off."

Caspar trotted over to look at them, and called to Jonty, "Mind if I go first?—just once." He took Ebony over the eight blocks, elegantly but at a properly cautious pace. Diana breathed worshipfully.

"Very ingenious," he said, rejoining them. "Different gaps all along, so you have to watch yourself. No, Diana, I was not wonderful, I was extremely slow."

"Oh, look!" said Diana, glowing.

Jonty had got her ride in line astern, and was leading them over the jumps. Sensibly, with the young ones to come, she took it unspectacularly. Lucy followed on Robert and Margaret on Gingerbread; neither horse was a jumper, but they were lively from the canter and knew the course well.

"Good, both of you," Valentine called. "Come on, Jane, ride him up; use your whip."

Jane used her whip and got round with some stumbles; Karen started well, was false-footed and then nearly ridden over by Benjamin, who came up flying and not wholly in control.

"Benjamin, *gently!*" And quietly behind her brother Bridie skipped neatly along without a fault.

"There were two more," said Caspar.

"They probably don't want to jump. Mark hasn't done much." The two who had not jumped were still by the gorse coverts, behind which the sun was setting in a haze of leaden lavender. "They can go round once more if they like, but it's a good twenty-five minutes back."

She had not raised her voice, but the young ones turned out of the jumping line, filing behind Bridie in unusual silence. "You can go round once more," Valentine called to them.

Jane said quietly, "The others are going now," and the three of them trotted gently across the road and lined themselves up as a front row of spectators. Benjamin wheeled Mouse to speak fast and urgently to Jonty. Jonty merely shook her head without looking at him, and with a white angry face Benjamin joined the audience, placing himself squarely in front of Valentine. She thought, but did not say, that Jonty was right; Benjamin at speed over the blocks was hardly safe to himself or anyone else in range.

Jonty led her line back down the road, waved it behind her, and gathering Fallada put him hard and savagely at the course.

"Lovely, lovely," breathed Diana.

Lucy followed at once, shrieking, "Go *on*, Bobs!" and before they were over and out Margaret slapped her whip on Gingerbread's shoulder and kicked him on. All three of them wheeled at speed back to their starting-point; but now there were two other horses in the line.

"Mark," said Valentine in apprehension. "I don't know if he can—"

Harvey knew the course too; he thundered relentlessly down it, Mark sitting grimly tight and not interfering.

"What's come over Mark? Last week he— Oh my God." The fifth horse was halfway through the course.

"Who's that? Oh, Sailor," said Caspar.

"Val, I didn't know Bobs and Gingerbread were jumpers," said Diana.

"Get them warmed up," said Caspar when Valentine did not answer, "and you won't know the laziest horse." Sailor cantered back to the start.

"Benjamin," said Valentine very quietly, "who is that riding Sailor?"

Without looking back at her Benjamin said, "Chris. Why not?"

Why not indeed? Chris had rescued Benjamin; Chris had been hailed as a hero; Chris had every reason to think himself welcome. To quieten herself Valentine stroked Barnaby's neck. Why should Chris not ride with them?

But she would not ride home at Chris's side. She could not.

They were coming in again, keeping up the speed, keeping the horses lively. Jonty was signalling with a hand above her head. What was she—? Oh, they were knotting their reins again; Jonty was going in to the jumps with her whip high above her head. And as they jumped the girls began to sing. In the clear evening air they sang with astonishing sweetness as each came up to the first jump. Jonty, Lucy, Margaret: *"O Fallada, my Fallada!—" "O Bobstacle, my Bobstacle!—" "O Ginger-bread, my Gingerbread!"*—all to the tune of *O Tannen-baum.*

The boys did not sing. Over went Sailor, Chris's meagre

little body balanced perfectly, his whip flourished; over went Mark, still with his reins, but riding hard and dourly. The five of them wheeled to the right, flashed through the gorse coverts, and turned at speed back on to the road.

"Not again, no!" said Valentine uncontrollably, and kicked Barnaby forward.

Benjamin said one word, and the four children turned their ponies broadside as a barrier in front of her.

She stared at them in astonishment, and Diana caught her arm.

"Look, look!"

"They've done jumping," Benjamin said flatly.

They had changed formation. Jonty, Chris, and Lucy were in line abreast, Margaret and Mark behind. They were coming at top speed directly down the track towards the bridge, and only Jonty was singing now, harsh and high and broken.

"O Fallada, O Fallada, if she could see you now!"

The horses, ridden up as they never were in their placid lives, were half wild. All that Valentine could see was Chris's staring face in the middle of the front line. She dragged Mouse's head aside and pushed Barnaby past him, and was pulled back by Caspar crying, "You'll be ridden down!"

The five horses thundered down on the bridge. Lucy, on the outside, pulled Robert out so late that he plunged wildly and she came off, rolling over and over. At the same moment Jonty leant over and lightly and neatly slapped Sailor with her whip on his neck. Sailor swerved from the blow, found his nose on the parapet of the bridge, and with a scream of hooves skidding on concrete arched his back to a trembling stop. Chris went over his head to the road below.

It was an accident; they all knew that it was an accident. It was only between Jonty and Caspar that this view was ever disputed. While Valentine and Diana were leading the steep scramble on foot down to the road where Chris lay still, Caspar made directly for Fallada and caught his rein.

"Why did you do that?"

Gently Jonty disengaged her rein and leant forward to put her hand on Fallada's crest and run it lovingly down his arched neck. It took a very close eye to see that she was slowly shuddering.

"He came back to ride with us. We don't ride with killers," she said.

CHAPTER 14

In the weeks that followed, Valentine harped incessantly upon Mr. Tidy.

"You don't understand," Diana said, to Caspar's eventual irritation at what he thought a side-issue. "Mr. Tidy's the only one involved who wasn't remotely to blame. She can feel quite simply sorry for him." She added after thought, "Well, the one who was least to blame. Didn't he know anything about his boy?"

"Considering the rest of the children involved," said Caspar precisely, "I don't think that that needs an answer."

"Yes it does," said Diana sadly. "If he had known, what could he have done about it?"

Finally, when Valentine's obsession began to approach the conviction that she should go and see Mr. Tidy, Caspar went himself.

"My mother," he explained carefully, looking unnaturally tall and neat in the neglected little kitchen cluttered with encrusted saucepans and crumby butter-papers, "my mother feels that it would be painful for you to see her, but she wished you to know that all her most

sympathetic thoughts are with you." That was not quite
how Valentine would have put it, but Caspar did not easily adopt another's style.

"Ah. Well now," said Mr. Tidy, who had shrunk lately:
"least said soonest mended, is what I always say."

"I'm sure you are right. But if there were anything my
mother or I could do—"

"No," said Mr. Tidy.

Elaborately, to smooth over embarrassment, Caspar en-
gineered his retreat towards the door. At the last possible
moment Mr. Tidy said, "They're talking of sending my
boy to this new hospital. Midlands somewhere, special.
They think they could do more operations and maybe
give him a bit more mobility. As they call it."

"I hope it will be successful."

"Take time, of course. Might look for a job up there
myself. Be with him, you know. Going up Monday."

"We should say goodbye, then?"

"Yes," said Mr. Tidy with relief. This established, he
mumbled, "Nice of you, coming. My best to your mum."

"Thank you, I'll tell her."

As they shook hands at the kitchen door, Mr. Tidy
brought out suddenly, "Don't hold anything against her,
tell her too. Brought it on himself. I know."

He at last met Caspar's eye.

"He was working for the Belton brothers, wasn't he?"
said Caspar. "Planning to steal my mother's horses, perhaps? Boasting about it to Jill?"

A wry smile curled Mr. Tidy's lips. "Of course he was
working for the Beltons," he said. "They're his uncles. His
mum was a Belton."

It was a sharp January afternoon, promising frost. Caspar walked home past Stumbletts, and stopped to watch
the children schooling in the meadow. Stirrups crossed
over their saddles, reins knotted, round and round they   N26

walked and trotted, laughing and calling across the circle. He picked out the familiar faces. In the centre Jonty sat Fallada, watching them with her faint ironic smile on her round face. She was singing to herself, very sweetly just above her breath, the tune of *O Tannenbaum* to words he could not hear.

About the Author

Kenneth O'Hara is a successful writer living in England. *Nightmares' Nest* is his first novel for the Crime Club.